CROSSED

Quentin Samuels

TABLE OF CONTENTS

Contents

Title Page

AUTHOR BIO

Prologue
1

Chapter 1
6

#CARTEL
6

Chapter 2
23

#SANTANA
26

#CARTEL
33

#SANTANA
35

Chapter 3
38

#CARTEL
38

#DE'ASIA
40

#RICHBOY
45

Chapter 4
47

#CARTEL
47

#RICO 56

Chapter 5 60

#SANTANA 60

#CARTEL 67

Chapter 6 76

#Detective Shaw 76

#RICHBOY 79

#DETECTIVE SHAW 81

Chapter 7 83

#CARTEL 83

#RICHBOY 86

#CARTEL 85

#JUVIE 95

#CARTEL 97

Chapter 8 100

#RICHBOY 100

Chapter 9 107

#SANTANA 107

#JUVIE

Chapter 10

115

#RICHBOY

115

#ALPO

120

Chapter 11

125

#CARTEL

125

#DE'ASIA

128

#CRACK HEAD NANCY

131

#JUVIE

132

#DE'ASIA

136

Chapter 12

146

#ALPO

146

#PARISH

148

Chapter 13

155

#SANTANA

155

#DETECTIVE SHAW

159

#SANTANA

160

#CARTEL

165

Chapter 14   168

#DETECTIVE SHAW   168

#RICHBOY   168

#DE'ASIA   172

#ALPO   173

Chapter 15   176

#DE'ASIA   176

Chapter 16   183

#RICHBOY   183

#ALPO   185

#RICHBOY   186

#DETECTIVE SHAW   189

Chapter 17   191

CARTEL   191

#DE'ASIA   192

#SANTANA   194

#PARISH   195

#CARTEL   196

AUTHOR BIO

Quentin Samuels, a little league baseball coach and the author of *Crossed Out,* was born and raised in Columbia, SC. He is a devoted father of five boys and a member of Brooklyn Baptist Church in Columbia, SC. Quentin is also an advocate for all who have become victims of their circumstances, whether educational or economical. He believes in creating a safe and nurturing environment where individuals can strive to reach their full potential regardless of their obstacles. Quentin is passionate about providing resources and support to empower people to take control of their lives and achieve success. Through his short stories and books, he inspires, motivates, and guides kids and their parents to break away from their everyday lives and enter a realm of new possibilities. His publications are essential for educators and parents who want to raise cultured, mindful, sensitive, compassionate, and socially and emotionally aware children.

Prologue

#BIG AL'

Twenty years in prison was a long time. It felt like I would never be released from this hell hole. I had only knocked down four years. I still had a decade to do. I laid in my bunk, listening to an old Master P. song. Music was like my lifeline. Music and books kept my mind off the fact that I used to be one of the biggest drug dealers in South Carolina before I was arrested.

Now I had nothing but a cellphone my old roommate left me when he was released a few months ago. I went from fucking any celebrity female, to no females at all. Females didn't respect what a mu'fucka used to do for them. They had bills to pay and kids to feed. A drug dealer with twenty years was only history.

A couple of females did hold me down for the first two years, though. But that shit didn't last too long. All it took was for another drug dealer with the money I used to have to get in their ear just like I used to do.

I was still listening to music when my son's mother called. I knew it had to be important because Vetta never called me before.

Usually, it would be my son calling, but he was locked up in Juvenile for drugs and a gun.

"Hello." I answered.

"Ali, how are you?" Vetta asked. She sounded sexy as hell.

"I'm maintaining, can't complain."

"That's good to hear."

"No need to ask about me. How's Jersey treating you?" I asked.

"You know how Paterson is—nothing's changed but the year. When's the last time you spoke to Cartel?" Cartel was our son. "That's what I called you about."

My heart sped up. "What do you mean? He okay?" I asked, sitting up in my bunk.

"Yeah, he's good. Still in Juvie."

(I sighed with relief) "Oh, then what's the problem?"

Vetta took a deep breath, then said, "Cartel not coming back to my house Ali. The boy is too grown. He want to sell them drugs on the corner, then that's where he need to be." Vetta spat.

"Vet, don't be like that. You know how it is out there. Don't give up on our boy."

"Ali, I washed my hands with him. He ain't going to change. That boy Willie just waiting to give Cartel some crack to sell." Vetta said.

"Willie Tucker, from Newark?" I asked.

"Yeah, he got a group of young boys running 'round here selling and killing. And I don't have the time for it, Ali. I'm sorry."

I could not believe this shit. My son was fifteen years old with no place to go. His mother had given up on him and I was locked up down south on a twenty-year bid.

"When he get out Vetta?" I asked.

"He'll get out next week, on the first of the month."

"Say no more" I ended the call without saying goodbye. Then I called Nina.

Nina was a lil' rider I used to run with when I was moving bricks in Carolina. I never had a sexual relationship with her, she was more like a sister. She would keep my dope a her spot from time to time, and that was it. But still, she owed me a few favors.

"Hello," she answered.

"Nina, what's good fam? It's been a while." I said.

"Big Al', this you?"

"Girl, you know my voice."

"How you been nigga? The streets miss you out here man. For real."

"I miss y'all too," I lied. I really was just trying to get my son in a good position. Nina was the only person I knew that was responsible and trustworthy. "But check this. I need a favor ma," I was jumping straight to the point.

"Run yo lips big bro."

"My baby moms kicked my son out. I need you to let him crash at yo' spot for second."

"Well, you know I live in the projects now. I'm not living on Second Loop Road no more," she said.

"Why you move?"

"Big Al you know I couldn't pay that rent. You paid that shit every month." We both burst out laughing.

"Yeah, that rent was high," I agreed.

"But he can come here if he like. Don't nobody live here but me."

"Okay. But I need one last favor."

"What?"

"I need you to pick him up from juvie."

"When?"

"On the first"

"Done," she replied.

After the phone call, I felt better. But I knew I would have to do more. I couldn't have my son living out there living with some mu'fuckas like some type of bum. And he damn sure wasn't working for nobody. The only choice I had was to give him the game, and of course telling him all of my mistakes.

Chapter 1

#CARTEL

It was no feeling better than the feeling I had stepping out of Juvenile. I felt like so much weight lifted off my shoulders. I searched the parking lot for my mother's truck, but it was nowhere to be found. Seconds later, a blue Honda turned into the parking lot. At first, I didn't think nothing because I knew my mother would never drive a Honda. Then the Honda stopped, and the window rolled down.

"You must be Cartel."

A dark-skinned woman said. I looked at her like she was crazy. "Who are you?"

"I'm Nina. Ali wanted me to pick you up. He on the phone," she said, sticking her IPhone out the window. The New Jersey sun shined like car headlights at night. I squinted my eyes and took the phone. "Hello?" I said into the phone.

"Son, how you been in there?" My dad asked.

"I've been good. You know how it is."

"Well, Nina like my sister. She going to take you down south with her."

"What do you mean down south? Where my mom's at?" I asked.

"Cartel, Vetta said you been causing too much trouble up there. She don't want you back over there." My father's words were like a knife to my soul. I haven't spoken to my mother since I was in juvenile, but I never thought she would wash her hands of me. (I wouldn't repeat this since vet said it that way in the start) "But don't sweat that Cartel. You will be okay," my father said.

"Man, I don't know nobody in the south. What the fuck ima do down there?" I asked with anger.

"Son, just give it a try. If you don't like it Nina will bring you back."

I thought about all my options. If I decided to stay in Jersey, then I wouldn't have a place to go. All my friends lived at home with their parents. As bad as I didn't want to go, I knew I had to go.

"Alright, I'll go. But I need to go get my clothes from mom's apartment," I said, walking over to the passenger seat. I got in the car and shut the door. The inside of the car smelled like a pound of marijuana.

"That's cool," my father said, "but I want you to go see an old friend of mine before you do anything."

"Who?" I asked.

"Her name is Ms. Anna May."

Ms. Anna May lived in Passaic, New Jersey, not too far from Paterson. I wasn't quite sure what I was going to see her for, but I trusted my father. Although he was locked up, he was very wise and his love for me was unconditional. I had millions of memories of my father when he was a free man. I could go on and on about the fun we had, but that was for another time.

Nina parked in front of Ms. Anna May's house. "I'll be out here," she said. I took a deep breath before I got out of the car. The house sat near a small church. There were plenty of houses on the street, but nobody was out. No cars were moving, and no animals were roaming around. It seemed like Nina and I were the only two in the world for a minute. It was like a ghost town, and that wasn't normal for Jersey.

I tapped on the door, but no one answered, so I tapped again. "Cartel Brown, come in," a raspy voice cracked through the air. I opened the door and stepped inside.

"Come sit down, son," Ms. Anna May said. I shut the door behind me. Ms. Anna May sat alone at a small table. We were in the living room, but there was no T.V. or couch in sight. The living room was dark. The only light came from two candles that sat aflame on the table.

"Sit, son," Ms. Anna May ordered. I sat across from her at the table. (No couch, but you could mention here that there were two chairs or something lurking in the shadows) Ms. Anna May was very old, she had to be every bit of eighty, at least. Her hair was the color of salt, and her skin shined in the candlelight like black diamonds.

"Joe and Betty Brown," she said, half smiling.

"Who?" I asked.

"Your grandparents," she whispered as she stared into my eyes. "They are guiding you, son. But you must listen and recognize it.

My grandparents had died before I was born. My father told me they had died from natural causes. He never explained in detail, and I never asked.

"They talk through your father sometimes. They send messages through Deon, too."

"Deon?" I asked.

"Deon Parker," she said. I knew exactly who Deon was, but I was wondering how she knew him. Deon was my best friend since first grade. Everybody called him Dough. At that moment, I realized she was reading me.

"You is a special kid, Cartel. But you must live according to your D.N.A., which is the basic chromosome material containing and transmitting the hereditary pattern." She slid me a folded piece of paper. "Don't open it until you are ready to live, and once you do, you may never reveal."

I didn't say anything, I just tucked the paper into my pocket.

"And this will protect you, son," she said setting a small vile on the table. It was red and filled with something liquid. "Never lose that. It is your wealth, protection and life. Go with your first mind, son, because your first mind is that of your ancestors. Sometimes a thought may seem bad, but always remember, the only person who was perfect was Jesus. So, live your life, son. Whatever you wanted to be yesterday, just be that Cartel. Be that through your natural D.N.A., which is on the paper."

Ms. Anna May spoke for another five minutes, and then I was released. For some reason, I felt like I had just left a church service.

The world outside looked different, even. People were running up and down the street like it was some type of holiday. I was fifteen with a fresh start.

-　　-　　-

On our way to my mother's apartment, I opened the paper. It had five lines. The first line read: *Allergic to gold. Colors attract energy and gold attracts negative energy to your D.N.A.*

The second line read: *Remain cool, calm and collected at all times. Never make decisions with your emotions.*

The third line read: *Organize everything. It will keep you on balance and in order.*

The fourth line read: *Give and you shall receive.*

And the last line read: *Respect love. This means to acknowledge when someone loves you, and never take it for granted.*

I read the paper multiple times before putting it back in my pocket

"What's that?" Nina asked.

"Nothing," I lied. "Turn left at the corner."

Nina stopped at the stop sign, and then turned left. "My mother lives right there," I pointed to the small apartment complex. "Park next to the white Tahoe," I said.

Nina did as she was told, and I got out of the car.

"Hey Cartel!" I heard a voice coming from somewhere beside me. "When you got out of Juvie?" Ms. Sally asked. She sat on her porch smoking a Newport.

"I got out today," I said, walking to my mother's door.

"Well welcome home. You bet' not go back."

"Thank you, Ms. Sally. I'm not going back," I promised. I knocked on my mother's door and she opened it.

"I told your father—" I cut her off mid-sentence.

"I'm just coming to grab my clothes. I'll be out in five minutes."

She stepped aside and I walked to my room.

"Everything is where you left it," she assured me. "I never went in there while you were gone."

I shut the door behind me and ran to my closet. I looked down and reached inside my Jordan sneakers. I smiled when I felt the cold steel. I grabbed the handle of my 22 pistol and put it in my back pocket.

Then I threw all my clothes in a black trash bag I found under my bed. I grabbed another bag and placed my shoes inside. Tying the bags up, I took them outside to Nina's Honda. She popped the trunk so I could put the bags inside. I placed them neatly in the trunk and slammed it shut.

"Nina, give me two seconds," I said, and then I rushed back inside.

My mother stood in the living room; her eyes were filled with tears. I rushed to my bedroom and snatched my phone from underneath my pillow. I looked around the room one more time before I walked out.

My mother was standing in the same spot, crying. I walked over to her and wiped the tears from her face. "I love you, ma," I said.

"I l-... love you too, son," my mother said, choking between her words. I kissed her on the forehead, and then I left.

The sun was starting to go down and the wind was beginning to blow. I got back in the car.

"We need to find somewhere to crash until morning," Nina said.

"That's cool. My partner, Willie, will let us sleep over there until tomorrow," I said.

"Where he live?"

"Pull out and make the next right."

Nina's cell phone went off as she pulled out of the parking lot. "Hello," she answered. "Here, yo pops want you," Nina said.

I took the phone from her and placed it to my ear. "What's good, pop?"

"How you feeling?" He asked.

"I'm good."

"That's what's up. I need you to do one more thing when you get a chance."

"What's that?"

"Go to a bookstore and grab a book."

"What's the name of it?" I asked, pointing Nina in the direction of Willie's house.

"The title is 'The Forty-Eight Laws of Power.' The author is Robert Greene."

"Say no more I'll get it when I can," I said.

"Alright. Call me when you settle down in Carolina."

"Bet." I ended the call and gave Nina back her phone.

"Pull in the next driveway," I said. Nina turned in and parked behind Willie's Charger. "Let me run inside and let him know what's up." Nina nodded her head and I got out of the car.

Willie lived in a two-story house with his girlfriend. I knocked on the door several times before he finally opened it.

"Damn nigga. You could've at least wrote a nigga," I joked.

"Welcome home, kid. I'm sorry, I been busy. You know how the money is," he said.

"It's cool. I'm home now."

"And you got big while you was in there," Willie said, sizing me up. I was brown skin and stood at 6'2". Most people said I looked like the rapper, The Game.

"Yeah, I been working out," I said.

"That's what's up. What you need though? You goin' to hit the block back up? I got fourteen grams left. Dough and Saint took the rest," Willie explained.

I looked back at Nina's Honda, then I looked back at Willie. "Nah, I'm leaving to go down south in the morning. Me and my people just need to lay here until then," I said.

"Damn, you leaving kid?" Willie asked, twisting his lips.

"Yeah, my mom's kicked me out. She said I was causing too much trouble."

"That's fucked up." Willie looked at the Honda.

"Who you got with you?" he asked.

"My pop's homegirl."

"Alright, you can fall back here. My wife won't be home 'til six in the morning. She working the graveyard shift."

I looked at the Honda and waved Nina inside. She grabbed a few things from the backseat, then stepped out.

"Oh, my God," Willie said, biting his bottom lip.

I looked a Nina good for the first time. She stood about 5'7" with beautiful black skin, and the body of a Goddess. Her blue Levi jeans hugged her thighs just right, and her hair was shoulder-length. She shut the car door and threw her purse over her shoulder. Nina noticed our reaction to her beauty. She cracked a smile, throwing her hips from left to right as she walked towards us.

"Hi," Nina said, looking at Willie.

"What's good? Come on in," Willie stepped aside, and Nina and I walked inside the house.

The inside of the house was massive. "Make yourself comfortable," Willie said, locking the door. "You hungry?" he asked.

"Hell yeah. I'm starving," I said. I flopped down on the living room sofa and Nina sat beside me. The sixty-inch flat screen was playing the news. My pistol was hurting my ass, so I took it from my back pocket and put it in my front pocket. I tapped my other pocket to make sure my vial was still there. I pulled it out and looked at it for a second, then I placed it back.

"Ima make some ham and cheese sandwiches," Willie said from the kitchen.

"That's fine big bro," I replied.

I was about to get comfortable when I thought about Dough and Saint. I needed to see them before I left for the south. "Yo Willie, Ima shoot up here to Main Street to see Dough and Saint real fast."

"No problem son, I know you need to see them before you leave," Willie said.

"Nina, I'll be back in a second. Willie's good people. Make yourself at home."

"Ok. Be safe out there, Cartel. Don't get into no trouble," Nina said. I smiled because she reminded me of my mother in so many ways.

"I won't," I said. Then I left out the side door. Main Street was only a few blocks from where Willie lived. I walked down the sidewalk and took Harriso Street straight down. Everything looked the same from when I left a year ago. Fiends were roaming, looking for their next hit, and drug dealers held the block down. On Main Street, the crack dealers' mindset was get paid by all means, and nobody embodied this attitude more than Dough and Saint, who were the youngest two on the block.

I spotted the two posted up on the wall of the Deli. Dough noticed me first and squinted his eyes. "Is that my boy?" he asked, pushing himself off the wall. Saint looked over and grinned. "Yeah, that's Cartel. I know that walk from anywhere son," Saint said.

I dapped them up, smiling from ear to ear. "I missed y'all niggas," I said.

"Nigga we missed you," Dough said, digging in his pocket. He pulled out a wad of cash and gave me a few hundreds. A split second later, Saint did the same.

"Good luck y'all," I said, stuffing the money in my pocket. "The game look lovely," I was talking about the drug game.

"Man, Dough and I really get our check from jacking these clowns out here," Saint said.

"Yeah, that's where the money at," Dough agreed.

"We robbed one nigga last month for ten grand," Saint bragged.

"Damn, that's mad bread," I said.

"And we did that in five minutes," Dough added.

I thought about what I could do with ten grand. I could cop half a brick of crack and rip Main Street into pieces. I could cop a half a brick of cocaine, but nobody knew how to cook crack like Pete. He knew a special recipe or something. Whenever he cooked crack, the fiends didn't want anything else but that. Dough always said it was the cocaine. Pete was dealing with a Columbian woman named Villian, and there were rumors on the street that she sold raw, uncut cocaine.

I kicked it with Dough and Saint for a while, but then it was starting to get late. "Let me get out of here. I'm crashing at Willie's spot for tonight, then I'm heading to South Carolina," I said, dapping them up.

"Don't come back, son. Jersey ain't got shit to offer but prison and death," Saint said.

"Listen to Saint, fam. Don't come back," Dough agreed.

"I'll be back to get y'all, though," I said.

"Yeah, do that," Saint said.

"Hell, I might call you as soon as I get my loot right," I assured them.

We shared a few laughs, and then I made my way back to Willie's house. I couldn't wait to taste that ham and cheese sandwich he made for me. My stomach was in my back. (im not sure this makes sense)

When I got to Willie's house, I thought I could hear Nina's voice. I sped walked up the stairs to see what was going on, and then I heard Willie.

"Bitch, stop acting like you don't want this dick!" He said.

"Please don't hit me no more. I won't tell no—" Nina's words were cut short.

"Shut the fuck up!" Willie snapped.

I grabbed my pistol from my pocket without hesitating. My palms were sweaty and my body became hot instantly.

"Now drop these fucking jeans!" Willie shouted.

I twisted the knob slowly with my left hand, clenching my pistol in my right. I eased the door open as Nina began to scream. The first thing I spotted when I opened the door was Willie's huge back. He had Nina pinned against the living room floor. He was so busy trying to rip Nina's jeans that he didn't hear me come in.

"Bitch, get your hands off me!" Willie said and he punched Nina in the face.

My heart was pounding when I raised my pistol.

"Yo Willie," I said, calm and collected.

Willie stopped and turned his head around. Before he realized what had happened, I sent a bullet to his face.

PAP! The 22 sounded like a firecracker. The bullet only grazed him, and he grabbed his face and stood up. I fired the second shot to his left leg.

"Fuck!" He grunted in agony. He buckled to his knees and looked up into my eyes. The gun was shaking in my hand. His blood dripped from his face and was starting to form a dark pool on the floor.

"You goin' to... kill me... for this bitch?" He said in between shaky breaths.

Nina stumbled to her feet as I got closer to Willie.

I was about to say something, but I decided not to, and I squeezed the trigger two more times directly in his face. His body jerked back, and he laid flat on his back right in his own living room. He choked on his blood as he tried to fight for his life. Nina spat in his face, then stumbled out of the house. I tucked my gun slowly and turned around. Before I left, I grabbed a half ounce of crack that sat on the table.

Chapter 2

#SANTANA

Money Bag Gang was one of the most organized gangs in Florence, South Carolina, with only eight members. Rico was the Head Nigga in charge. He only stopped by the Projects once in a blue moon. If he was in town, then everyone knew something major was about to go down.

Wayne was the Captain of the Money Bag Gang. He controlled all the movements in the Oakland Heights Projects. If anything was wrong in the Money Bag operation, Rico would get on Wayne and Wayne would get on us.

Wayne was not the one to fuck with; he was a very serious mu'fucka. When a member got out of line, Wayne showed no pity. The individual would be punished and dealt with accordingly. Wayne was very quiet and direct. When he spoke, the Gang knew it was something they needed to know.

Next in line was me, Santana Paul. I was the Lieutenant, and I played my position well. I was the recruiter and money operator. I controlled who became a member of the Money Bag Gang. It was Rico, though, who decided who would move up in rank. He made his decisions based off of our weekly reports. Once a week, the Gang turned in a paper with the weekly activities, shootings, fights, penalties and money earnings. I also collected the money and counted it, so it would be ready for Wayne when he did his rounds on Monday mornings.

Trouble was the Sergeant. He was the bookkeeper and designated driver. He had the easiest job, but it was also the wackest one. He couldn't drink or smoke because he always had to be prepared to drive or write. If the book was fucked up at the end of the week, Wayne would make sure that Sergeant was fucked up, too. All incidents and incomes needed to be right and exact.

Kapo and Turk were the Enforcers, or security. They guarded the Projects with their lives. If anything moved wrong, then they were to alert the runners and or take action on the situation. They also did most of the dirty work.

At the bottom of the ranking system were Cam and Juvie. They operated out of an apartment in the Projects. They did hand-to-hand transactions all day, and they also made short runs. If they had a sell within a five-block radius, then they could deliver. Anything outside of the five-block radius was not our territory.

Other gangs or organizations operated in North Florence. Rich Squad was a small group of just four dudes who sold crack on Brunson Street. We had an unspoken agreement with them to respect other peoples' territory. That meant we never spoke about it, but we all knew what was up.

There was another drug gang known in North Florence as Loud Pack Pushers. They only served marijuana, so they weren't any competition for us. They were allowed to distribute their product freely. I had Zack on speed dial, over at the Loud Pack Pushers. He was my weed supplier.

With all the drugs floating around the North Side, there were a lot of violent crimes being committed. The murder rate in Florence was at an all time high. Fiends were burglarizing peoples' home to come up with a dime, and the Jack Boys were always plotting. North Florence was a concrete jungle and only the strong could survive, while the weak folded like paper.

#CARTEL

The ride to South Carolina was spent mostly in silence. I couldn't believe I had murdered

Willie. He was like an O.G. to me, but at the same time, I knew he deserved every bullet I sent his way. Raping a female was a big no-no in my book, especially someone that my father sent to help me.

When we made it to Washington, Nina stopped at a motel. "Cartel, I need some rest bad. And I know you wanna get some rest yourself," she said.

"Yeah, that's cool," I said.

Nina opened the car door, but before she got out, she looked back at me.

"Thanks for what you did back there, Cartel," she said.

"No problem," I said. She got out of the car, and we checked into a room.

"Ima get in this shower," Nina said.

"Alright. I'll get in after you. I need to get out of these clothes." I threw my bag on the floor and took my gun out from my pocket. I placed my gun with the dope inside my bag of clothes. Then I took my vial out from my pocket and placed it under my pillow. It was damn near midnight at this point, but I wasn't tired. I grabbed the piece of paper Ms. Anna May gave me, and I read it again. I knew the words on the paper by heart now, so I threw it in the trash.

There were two beds in the room, and I took the one closer to the door. I flopped down on the bed to relax, while Nina was in the shower.

Somehow, I dosed off. When I woke back up, Nina was asleep in her bed. I looked down at my phone and it was nine o'clock in the morning. I decided to get up and take a long, hot shower. It was the hottest shower I took in a while. I cleaned my body good, then I dried off. I brushed my teeth with the Aim toothpaste sitting on the motel sink. Then, I got dressed. I put on a pair of blue jeans and a fresh white t-shirt. I laced my icy, white Air Forces.

Nina was still sleeping, so I grabbed my vial and my gun, and I took a walk. I was locked down for too long to be sitting up in a motel. I had to move around.

I walked across the street to a Burger King, where I ordered a burger and some fries. I was starving. I smashed the food in two bites, then flushed it down with a large Sprite. I was sitting by myself enjoying my new freedom when I spotted a bookstore. I threw my trash away and rushed over to the bookstore.

The store was busy early. I walked up to an employee. He was a young white man with a low cut.

"How may I help you?" he asked.

"Um, I'm looking for a book by Robert Greene."

"What's the title?"

"'Forty-Eight Laws of Power.'"

"Hold on one second." He walked off for a minute and brought the book back. I took the book. It was blue and orange with the word *Power* written vertical in the center of the cover.

"That's a nice book," he said. I ignored him as I flipped through the pages. It had chapters each dedicated to a different law. The first Law of Power read:

Never Outshine the Master.

Then underneath it read:

Always make those above you feel comfortably superior. In your desire to please or impress them, do not go too far in displaying your talents, or you might accomplish the opposite.

Then it broke down how the person above may begin to fear you or feel insecure. It explained how that could be dangerous, and I understood it all immediately. I loved it.

"I'll buy it," I said. The man cashed me out, then I left the bookstore.

I was on my way back to the room when two police officers approached me.

"Sir, where are you coming from?" the taller of the two asked.

"The bookstore over there," I replied.

"Well, we received a call from that bookstore that a black male was stealing."

"Get the fu—" I stopped mid-sentence and thought about the paper that Ms. Anna May gave me. One of the lines read: *cool, calm and collected.* I took a deep breath and recollected my thoughts.

"Sir, I just bought this book," I said, showing him 'Forty-Eight Laws of Power'. I thought about my pistol and my heart sped up. All they had to do was search me and I was going to jail for a gun charge and quite possibly a murder charge. I would never see the streets again.

"By Robert Greene," the other officer said. "I read that book a few years ago. It's a pretty deep book. He wrote some other books you might want to check out after that one."

Before I could respond, the employee that helped me stepped out of the bookstore.

"Sir, it's not him. The man is still in there," the employee said.

"I'm sorry son," the officers said, and then they both went inside to arrest the thief.

"Let me get the fuck off these streets," I muttered to myself.

#SANTANA

I turned onto Oakland Heights and drove my black-on-black F-150 to the back. I never parked in front of the Projects. Females would pass by the Projects and see my truck, and then turn in to look for me. Oakland Heights wasn't really the Projects. It was an apartment complex, but to everyone on the North Side, it really seemed like the Projects. The real Projects, however, was just a few blocks away, where the Loud Pack Pushers operated.

Oakland Heights was a one-way-in, one-way-out apartment complex. (do you mean driving?) I parked my F-150 next to Trouble's car and killed my engine. I checked my face in the rearview mirror. I licked my lips and straightened the green bandana I wore around my low-cut fade.

I was light-skin with curly hair and green eyes. Most mutherfuckers mistook me for a pretty boy or the soft type because of my looks, but when they saw the green bandana, they knew I wasn't one to fuck with. Everyone in Florence knew that the green bandanas symbolized the Money Bag Gang. They also knew that the Money Bag Gang was responsible for almost half of the city's murders.

I was about to get out of the truck, when two of my friends rushed up.

"Yo Santana, give us something for fifty? Cam and Juvie, they ain't got nothin goin on right now," Mike said, scratching his face. I opened my door.

"Don't nobody got nothing right now. The work will be in later. And stop pulling up on my whip," I said, stepping out onto the hot concrete.

"Alright. Let us know when the shit hit man. Mu'fuckas starving," Big Ben said walking off, disappointed. I locked my truck and walked over to the apartment that we operated out of. I tapped the door two times slowly. Two slow knocks indicated that it was somebody from the Money Bag Gang.

Juvie opened the door. "Money what's good?" Juvie said, dapping me up.

"Still waiting on the work to drop." I stepped inside and locked the door back.

"Money, mad smokers been pulling up. Where the fuck Wayne at?" Cam asked me. We called one another 'Money,' just like Crips called one another 'Cuz.'

"Y'all know Wayne gonna pull up whenever Rico hit 'em with it. Money aint gon' hesitate to bring the work," I said. I dapped Trouble up, then I dapped Cam up. They both were playing Madden on the PS4. Everybody was waiting for the work to drop, but it wasn't going to happen until Rico showed. And it was suicidal to call him about the work.

I sat down on the couch and smoked a Newport. I inhaled the smoke, then exhaled slowly. The smoke felt good filling up my lungs. "Damn, y'all know what I just thought about?" I asked.

"What?" Cam asked, looking at me.

"Today is De'Asia birthday. Rico may not bring that work until later."

"Oh yeah. I forgot about that," Trouble said.

De'Asia was Rico's daughter, and she was turning seventeen. I was on my second pull from the Newport when Nina pulled up in her Honda. "Damn, where the fuck she been?" I thought to myself as I stood.

#CARTEL

"I thought you lived in the Projects," I said. Nina parked her car and took her key out of the ignition.

"Well, it's not really the Projects, but that's what we call it," she said. I noticed a few crackheads huddled up like they were plotting something. If they weren't crackheads, then they sure looked like they could go for some. Their clothes were two times bigger than they were, and their shoes looked like they had seen more action than most could speak for.

Nina and I got out of the car. "Pop the trunk," I said. When she did, I noticed a pretty Ricky-looking dude approaching.

"Nina, how you been living baby girl?" the dude asked, puffing a Newport.

"I'm good, Santana. How you?" Nina asked, locking her door.

"I'm maintaining," Santana paused, then asked, "What happened to yo' lip?"

"It's a long story."

Santana cut his eye at me, then followed Nina inside her apartment. I grabbed my bag and went inside the apartment. "Cartel, your room is upstairs," Nina said.

"Ok." I shut the door, then walked up to the room. There was only one bedroom upstairs, so I knew it was the one she was talking about. It was a nice sized room, with a queen size bed. There was a wooden dresser by the window. I put my bag in the corner and sat down on the bed. I took my 22 out from my pocket and placed it under my pillow. I was eager to read some more of the 'Forty-Eight Laws of Power', so I grabbed it from my bag. I sat back on the bed and started from where I left off. The book broke down the first law in multiple ways. I was about to enter the next chapter when someone knocked on my door.

"Come in," I said. The door opened and Santana peered inside.

"Money what's good? I can come in?" he asked.

"Yeah, I ain't doing nothing but reading."

He closed the door behind him. "What you reading?" he asked. I closed the door and handed it to him. He looked at the cover, then at me.

"How old are you?" he asked.

"Fifteen."

"A brother gave me this book when I was sixteen, but I never read it." Santana flipped through the pages, then placed it back in my hand. "You got a lot of heart for a fifteen-year-old." I looked at him hard to see what he was getting at. "Nina told me what you did back there in Jersey," he said.

"What?" I asked, twisting my lips.

"You good Money. You don't have to worry about that situation getting spread around. Nina just know she can tell me." Santana paused for a second, then he said, "If you need somethin' let me know. Nina is like my aunt. My mother and her were good friends back in the day."

Santana was a cool dude, and I could tell he was getting to the money. His gold teeth and Jesus piece charm spoke for him. "Yo Santana, Big Ben want to know if you got some work yet?" Nina yelled from downstairs.

"Man, I just told these mu'fuckas I ain't got no crack," Santana said to me. "These mu'fuckas aggravating," he added.

"I got a lil' bit," I said, remembering the fourteen grams in my bag.

"Yeah?" Santana asked, surprised.

I nodded my head and grabbed the half ounce from my bag. "Yo Nina, tell Big Ben to come up," Santana said, then looked at me. "Listen, it's no work in the Projects right now, so you can give these fiends whatever and they gon' take it," he said before Big Ben made it upstairs.

"Bet," I said. Upstairs in Nina's apartment, I sold my first slab.

Santana's phone went off and he answered it. "Talk to me Money." Someone on the other end said a few words and then he said, "I got you." Santana hung up the phone. "My people's daughter having a Project party tonight. It's her seventeenth birthday, you gon' party with me?" he asked.

"Where's it at?" I asked.

"Out here in the Projects. The whole North Florence gon' be out here," he said. I thought about it for a second. "And I'll make sure you get rid of the rest of that work," Santana added. How could I say no to that? I was selling fiends twenty-dollar slabs for thirty bucks.

"Yeah, I'll be out there," I said.

"Welcome to the North Side fam," Santana said as he dapped me up.

Chapter 3

#CARTEL

That night, I got myself prepared for the party. I put on my Kobe Bryant jersey, which was purple and yellow. My shorts were army fatigue, and I sported my purple and yellow LeBron James sneakers. I checked myself in the mirror Nina had on the bedroom wall. It was the first time I put on a real fit since my release from Juvenile.

Once I was ready to party, I called my father. He answered on the first ring. "What's up Pop?" I asked, sitting down on the bed.

"Same ol' shit back here son. Just a different day," he said.

"I feel you. Keep your head up back there."

"Cartel!" Nina yelled from downstairs.

"Hold up Pop. What's good Nina" I shouted back downstairs.

"Mike comin' up," she said.

"Alright. Send him on up here," I said. Seconds later Mike stepped in the room smelling like garbage.

"Yo Cartel, let me get aa gram for seventy-five," he said, with hope in his eyes.

"Son you know there ain't no work in the Projects," I said, letting him know that I was aware of what was going on, and he wasn't getting one over on me.

"Come on Nephew don't do me like that," Mike said.

"Ima do it for you one time. Next time Ima need the whole dollar." Dollar was another way to say one hundred dollars. I popped off a gram of crack and we made the transaction. He was smiling from ear to ear, revealing his coffee-stained teeth. "Thanks Nephew," Mike said as he ran back downstairs.

I placed my money on the bed, then I tied my dope back up. I only had seven grams left because Santana was sending sells here back-to-back. All the sells were twenties and better. I was about to get up, then I remembered my father was still on the phone. "Hello," I said into the phone.

"Yeah, I'm still here," he said. He didn't say anything about the transaction, but I was pretty sure that he heard it.

"I got that book too," I let him know.

"That's good, but don't just read the book, son. You have to study the laws and implement them into every second of your life," my father paused, then he asked, "do you still have the paper Ms. Anna May gave you for your D.N.A?"

"No, but I can recite the lines verbatim."

"Good, because that with the 'Forty-Eight Laws of Power' will give you crazy power, son. For real," he chuckled.

"I got you Pop. Be safe over there. I love you."

"I love you too, son. Oh, and Cartel," he said before I ended the call.

"Yeah?" I said.

"Always remember these three words: love, money and happiness. Every move you make in life should be another move closer to one of the three." I thought about the three words for second and how they all seemed to relate to one another. Money wasn't anything without love, love would be stressful without money, and love without happiness just didn't add up.

"I understand Pop."

#DE'ASIA

Today was my seventeenth birthday, and I was trying to turn up. My best friend Parish and I were smoking with our boyfriends, Richboy and Alpo. They were both brothers who were a part of a small drug gang called Rich Squad. Richboy and I met through Parish and Alpo, who were together for six months. Well, they were on-and-off for six months. One month Alpo was with Parish and the next he was with his baby momma. They had a very rocky relationship that was built on lies.

Richboy and I were together, but he wasn't really my type. He was too loud and full of drama. Parish was the only reason that I was trying to make it work. She was always saying something like "De'Asia, Richboy is a good man. You just have to give him time." But I was just about out of time. I was seventeen, and I wanted a real man. Or at least a man I was attracted to.

"Damn Parish, pass the blunt," Alpo joked.

"Hell, I only got two pulls nigga," Parish pulled on the blunt again.

"Puff, puff, pass," Alpo laughed at his own joke.

"Baby girl, you ever holla'd at your dad for me?" Richboy whispered in my eat.

"Yeah, I spoke to him the other night," I lied.

"And what did he say?"

"Um… he never gave me an answer. He just ignored me. He is very strict about his business."

"Man, yo' pops buggin'," Richboy snapped. That was the last straw for me. I couldn't deal with him any longer. I stood up from the couch and looked over at Parish. "Girl, let's go," I said, storming out the door. I got in my Lexus and waited for Parish to come out of the house. I pushed the horn so she would hurry up. A minute later, she exited the house and got in the passenger seat.

"What happened in there?" Parish asked. I backed out of Richboy's yard and headed home. "De'Asia, will you please tell me what happened back there?" Parish asked again.

"He keep aggravating me about asking my father if he can cop some drugs from him. I am not asking my father no crazy shit like that." I waited on Parish to respond, but she never did. She made me feel like she thought I was suppose to ask my father something crazy like that. I made a right on Irby Street. Ten minutes later, I turned into my father's driveway and parked behind his Range Rover.

"You don't have anything to say?" I asked.

"I'm saying De', Richboy is your boyfriend. He try'na come up, and your pop's the damn plug," Parish explained. I couldn't believe my best friend was taking a man's side. But then again, she always let dick control her mind. She was a pretty girl, but for some reason she was insecure. I rolled my eyes and got out of the car.

"I'm about to go get ready for my party," I said, trying to get her out of my sight for a while.

"Alright. I'll just meet you at the party then," she said. She shut my car door then walked over to her Crown Vic and sped out of my driveway.

I walked into the house and locked the door behind me. My father and I lived together in a two-story house. He was always on the move, so I had the house to myself the majority of the time. But since today was my birthday, he wasn't moving any drugs. He always stopped selling drugs for one day out of every year to make time for me. I was the only thing that mattered to him on this day.

"Baby girl, that's you?" My pops asked from upstairs.

"Yeah, it's me, daddy."

"Come up here. I have something for you."

"Comin' now," I said as I put my keys on the kitchen table and rushed up to his room. When I opened the door, he was sitting on the bed, counting money.

"Parish with you?" he asked., putting the stack of money down.

"No, she had to go get dressed for the party tonight."

"That's what's up." My father pulled out a jewelry box and gave it to me.

"What's this?" I asked, blushing.

"Open it."

I opened it and I was almost blinded by the diamonds shining out at me. "Damn, daddy," I said, counting the diamonds in the necklace.

"Happy Birthday, baby girl." He smiled, revealing his gold teeth.

"Thanks, daddy." I hugged him and kissed him on the cheek. Then I looked at the necklace again. It was all gold with a heart charm. On the back, it had baby girl carved in cursive. It was the best give I had ever gotten.

#RICHBOY

"Yo Alpo, call shawty back to make sure that's still a go. I ain't got no time for no blank mission," I warned my brother. He pulled out his phone and called Parish. She answered.

"Love, where you at?" Alpo asked. She said something that I couldn't hear. Then he answered, "Okay. Everything still, everything right. Say no more."

Alpo ended the call and smiled. "It's a go my nigga. She said she gon' give us the scoop on the nigga when he leave the party. All we got to do is follow the nigga home."

"Why she just can't give us the nigga address and we just break in the nigga spot while he gone? Hell, the drugs are in the house, not in his whip," I said.

"Nigga, Rico probably got a safe that have to scan his eyes just to open. He ain't got no bricks in a Jordan shoebox in his closet," Alpo laughed. He always tried to cut jokes.

"Fuck you," I spat.

"Yeah, yeah, yeah. Call Vick and Lil-Baby. Tell'em to bring everything over to Brunson Street so we can be ready whenever she calls."

I dialed my cousin Lil-Baby's cell.

"Rich', tell the nigga to bring the AK's and the MAC's," Alpo said.

"Alright," I said. After about four rings, Lil-Baby picked up. "Talk to me, cuz," he said.

"Lil-Baby, I want you and Vick to bring everything to Brunson Street. We got some shit going down tonight," I said.

"Y'all want us to bring everything, everything?" Lil-Baby asked.

"Nigga, bring every single one," I answered.

"Bet. Me and Vick will be over in thirty minutes."

I ended the call and sat back. All we had to do now was wait. I was hoping De'Asia was there when we got there. I wanted to put a cap in her ass, too, since she didn't want to plug me in. My dick would get hard just off of seeing that bitch bleed. I could already feel it coming just thinking about it.

Chapter 4

#CARTEL

The entire Projects were filled from the front to the back. Females were everywhere I looked, and they came in all shape, size and color. Redbone, black, brown, white, fat, thick, old, young and beautiful. The sight was amazing.

Santana and I were posted in the front of Nina's spot, bobbing our heads to a Yo Gotti track. "Yo money, you smoke trees?" Santana asked, showing me a kush-filled blunt.

"Nah," I said.

He pulled out his lighter and sparked it. I was still bobbing my head up and down when a group of guys walked up sporting green bandanas.

"What's poppin' money?" Santana asked, dapping the crew up.

"Man, where you been hiding?" one of the men asked Santana.

"Cartel, this is the Gang my nigga," Santana said, introducing me to the Money Bag Gang.

"What's up bro? I'm Trouble, and this is Juvie, Cam, Turk and Kapo," Trouble said, then gave me a dap.

"I'm Cartel." I dapped up the rest of the crew and posted back against the apartment building.

"Money, this shit's lit," Trouble said, looking at all of the women.

Santana passed the blunt to Turk, who took a long drag. "Cartel, you still got work?" Santana asked.

"Nah, I'm out."

Santana waved a crackhead back and he turned around pouting like a baby. Santana's phone went off then, and he answered it, "What's up money?" He looked at the crew and then told the caller, "Alright." He hung up the phone and put it back in his pocket.

"That was Wayne. Rico wants to see us at the spot," Santana said.

The crew turned to leave, but I stayed posted. Santana looked at me.

"What?" I asked.

"Money, come on," he said. The rest of the crew looked at Santana, then back at me. A split second later, I was mobbing with them through the crowd. We walked inside an apartment where two men and a girl sat at the kitchen table. I was the last one to walk in, so I locked the door and then followed them up to the table.

The table was small, so most of us stood around. The girl and I locked eyes almost immediately. She was the most beautiful girl I had ever seen. She had brown skin with long hair and sparkling eyes. Her lips were pink and glossy from her lip gloss. I broke off eye contact with her and made a mental note to get her phone number when this was all over.

"Well, as you all know, today is my baby girl's bornday," a big man said.

"Happy Birthday De'Asia," Santana said. Then the rest of the crew followed, "Happy Birthday De'."

Santana pulled out a wad of hundreds and slid it across the table. De'Asia took the money. "Thanks, Santana," she said, showing off her deep dimples as she smiled.

"You're welcome," he said.

Santana caught Wayne staring at me. "Wayne, Rico, De'Asia, this is Cartel," he said.

"What, he a new runner?" Wayne asked.

"Yeah."

I looked at Santana like he was a fool.

"Hi Cartel, I'm De'Asia. Nice to meet you," De'Asia said, catching me off guard and making me forget everything Santana just said.

"Hi, and Happy Birthday. I would've gotten you something, but I didn't know it was your birthday until just now," I said.

"It's okay. Maybe you can make it up to me later?"

"My pleasure."

De'Asia nodded her head, then looked over at her father, who was staring at her. Then everyone burst out laughing.

"Damn, you gon' pimp my baby girl right in front of me?" Rico joked.

"Nah, you have a beautiful daughter. I'll never try to pimp her."

"I'm just messing with you youngin'. How old are you?" Rico asked.

"Fifteen. I'll be sixteen in a month," I added.

"You from up top somewhere?"

"Yeah, I'm from Jersey."

"I can tell," Rico pulled out a cigar and sparked it. "You remind me of a cat I used to run with some years back. He in the Joint now doing a lil' bid," Rico said.

"Ali Brown?" I asked.

Rico looked at me harder. "Yeah, we called him Big Al'," he said.

"That's my father," I said.

Rico stood up and walked over to me. "Man, you was this tall the last time I saw you," he said, holding his palm a little lower than his waist. "Yo pops was like my right-hand, until some shit popped off between me and some niggas from off Brunson Street." Rico paused, and then said, "Yo pops was from Brunson Street, and I was hustlin' out here in Oakland Heights. We still trapped together, though, and when he beef popped off, yo pops had to choose. He chose Brunson Street."

There was an awkward silence for a second. Then Rico said, "Soon after that, Big Al' got locked up."

I didn't know what to say. "Ronda Anderson your mother?" Rico asked.

"No, Vetta is my mother."

"Oh yeah, that's the one from Jersey. You're right," he said.

"Y'all make sure you treat lil' homie like family. His pops was a well-respected hustler out here on the North Side," Rico added. Then he hugged me tight.

"Welcome to the family homie," Santana said, then dapped me up.

"Hold up," Wayne said. Everyone looked at Wayne and Wayne looked at Rico.

"Oh yeah. Repeat after me, son," Rico said, looking down at me. "I promise to respect Money Bag Gang," he said.

"I promise to respect Money Bag Gang."

"I promise to be loyal to my brothers and never put anything before them."

"I promise to be loyal to my brothers and never put anything before them."

"And if I do, I shall pay with my life."

"And if I do, I shall... pay with... my life," I stuttered.

"Money Bag Gang for life," Rico said.

"Money Bag Gang for life," I repeated. Then Santana handed me a money green bandana.

"Welcome to the family money," Wayne said, standing to his feet. For some reason, it all felt right, and I enjoyed the moment.

Turk popped the top on a bottle of Goose and took a sip. He passed it to me. I took a swallow, then I took another.

"I'm hungry as a muthafucka," Rico said.

"Nina and them been finished with the food. They got all type of shit over there," Wayne said, licking his lips.

"Yeah, I'm about to go grab me a plate." Rico stood up and walked out the front door. Turk passed the bottle back to me and followed Rico.

"Money, you chillin' in here?" Santana asked me, cutting his eye at De'Asia. She was sitting at the table with her face in her phone.

"I'll be out in a second," I said. The rest of the crew stepped outside, leaving me alone with De'Asia. "Ma, you drink?" I asked, placing the bottle on the table.

She put her phone away and grabbed the bottle. "What bring you down here?" She asked.

I sat down across from her. "My mom kicked me out, so my pop sent me down here with his home girl, Nina," I said.

De'Asia took a sip and then slid the bottle across the table. "So, you a bad boy?" She wanted to know.

"Nah," I laughed. "I just be trying to get money."

"You a hustler?"

"Yeah, you could say that." I took a sip and passed the bottle back.

"After hustlin', do you have any other plans?" De'Asia asked.

She caught me off guard. "To be honest, I never thought past hustling," I said.

"Well, what do you like to do?"

I thought for a second, then I said, "I want to own my own business one day. Maybe like a clothing store or something."

"I can see that," she said, starting to slur her words a bit. I could tell the liquor was kicking in. I took the bottle and put the cap back on it. I was feeling quite good myself. "Tell me about you," I said.

"Well, I'm in twelfth grade. I graduate next year."

"That's what's up, ma!"

"And I want to be an author," she said.

"Author?" I asked.

"Yup. I want to write hood novels."

"I used to read them hood novels in Juvenile."

"Which ones have you read?" she asked.

"I read all the Cartel books and I read 'Death Around the Corner' by C-Murder."

"Them Cartels were good," she said.

De'Asia and I sat there for a while after that, and we talked about everything in the world. I found out her mother passed away from lung cancer when she was eleven. She and her mother were very close, more like sisters than mother and daughter. When we were done talking, the Projects were empty, and I was more than tired.

"I had a good time with you tonight," I said as I was getting ready to leave.

"I did, too," she said.

"When Ima see you again?"

"Whenever, just call me," she said, giving me her number.

#RICO

As I turned out of the Projects and headed home, I pulled out my cell phone and called Detective Shaw. He answered.

"I thought y'all was going to meet me in the Projects?" I asked.

"We're behind you muthafucka." I looked in my rearview mirror and seen his headlights.

"Bet," I said, and ended the call. I turned my music up a little to vibe to the beat. I was almost home when Detective Shaw called my phone back.

"What's up?" I asked.

"This car is following you with like four people inside. Ima pull them over," he said. I looked in my rearview again and saw the other vehicle.

"Alright, get their names and meet me at my spot," I said.

He hung up. I made a left on Irby Street and got in the right lane. I saw Detective Shaw hit his lights, making the vehicle pull over. I laughed to myself and kept it pushing. Minutes later, I turned in my driveway.

I got out of my Range Rover. I slammed the door and locked it. The night air was cold, and I couldn't wait to get into the house. Once I was inside, I turned on the living room light. "I wonder who the fuck was following me?" I thought to myself. It was probably some niggas that scoped me out at the party.

Detective Shaw knocked on my door about ten minutes later. "Come in bro," I said, sitting on my leather sofa. Shaw walked in with his partner, Hicks, behind him.

"Man, they jumped out and ran. But they left these," Shaw said, stepping aside. Detective Hicks held two black AK's on his shoulder.

"Damn, you ain't get no face?" I asked.

"Rico, I ain't on duty. I ain't have time to do all that. But they looked like the same, young black boys," Shaw said. He took a blue backpack from his back and placed it in my lap.

"How much is this?" I asked, unzipping the backpack.

"We confiscated three kilos. That's two and a half," Shaw said.

"Where the other half?"

"Man, give me my paper," Shaw spat.

I looked at Shaw with a mean mug, I wanted to kill that cracker. He had a slick mouth. "I'm only doing a few more runs and then I'm out. I ain't doing this shit no more," I reminded Shaw. I pulled out a wad of hundreds and placed it in his hands.

"And then what Rico? What you gonna do?" he asked.

"Move out of the state. I did this shit too long."

"Yeah, picture that," Shaw laughed and followed Hicks to the door.

"Damn, you can't leave the choppas?" I asked.

"Fuck you Rico," Shaw said, walking out and slamming my front door.

Shaw and I have been doing business for the last decade. After he first bust me, he found a brick of cocaine and two 9mms. But instead of taking me to jail, he made me buy a kilo from him. He started coming to me just about every week after that with bricks and guns. He would raid a drug spot in the West, East or South Florence, and sell me whatever he had for the low. Sometimes he would sell me a kilo of pure cocaine for five grand even. I would whip it into crack and give it to the Gang for four hundred an ounce. I was eating like a muthafucka.

I put the dope away and went to my room. I planned on whipping the two and a half kilos to four bricks of crack tomorrow. But by tomorrow night, every ounce would be gone out into the Projects.

That's just the way things went out here. But this whole scene was just about over for me. I knew I couldn't sell dope forever, and it was just a matter of time before the Feds came knocking on my door.

Chapter 5

#CARTEL

I woke up the next morning a little later than I normally did. Before I got out of the bed, I recited the laws to my D.N.A. Then I read a couple of pages out of the 'Forty-Eight Laws of Power'. I reread the eleventh law, which said, "Learn to keep people dependent on you." It broke the law down a little by saying that to maintain your independence, you must always be needed and wanted. I dwelled on the law for a while, then I hopped out of bed.

I got in the shower and did my usual hygiene routine. I was putting on my clothes after the shower when I heard someone knocking at the door. "Hold up," I said. I put my feet in my Jordans and grabbed my green bandana. I tied it around my wrist and then walked downstairs.

"Who is it?" I asked.

"De'Asia." I opened the door. She stood there looking better than the day before. "You ate breakfast?" she asked.

"Nah."

"Can I take you?"

"Yeah, I'll be right out." I rushed back up the steps and grabbed my vial. I put it in my pocket, and then I grabbed my phone, too. I thought about grabbing my pistol, but then I decided to leave it. On my way out the door, I stopped by Nina's bedroom and put a few hundreds on her bed. I wasn't sure where she was, but I knew she would spot the money whenever she returned home.

Once I got in the passenger seat of De'Asia's Lexus, she backed out of the parking spot and drove out of the Projects. "Everybody must still be asleep," De'Asia said, noting all the empty streets.

"Yeah, they probably tired from last night."

"You had fun?" De'Asia asked.

"I'm just glad I got to meet you ma."

She smiled, then made a left onto the highway. "You're so sweet," she said.

Seconds later, she turned into the parking lot of a restaurant. The sign on the front of the building read "Thunder Bird."

"Ma, this look like some country spot," I laughed.

"Trust me, they serve the best breakfast around," she said as she parked between a Jeep and a box Chevy on twenty-four-inch rims.

I got out of the car, and she followed me inside. Although I didn't know the restaurant like she did, I still didn't feel like she was supposed to lead the way. Leading was a man's job. I chose a table in the far back of the place. It looked like the restaurant was filled with old folks.

The restaurant was buffet-style, so I walked over to the food and made myself a big plate. I had grits, sausage, and eggs with extra cheese. I glanced over at De'Asia.

"Baby, you better stop being shy and fill that plate up," I said, looking at the fruit on her plate. She rolled her eyes at me, and then added eggs and grits to her plate.

- - -

#SANTANA

"Aawww… fuck me… Santana!" LaLa screamed as I threw my dick so deep in her stomach.

"This what you want bitch?" I pounded her harder. She laid on her back, with her legs spread eagle style. "Bitch, this what you want?" I asked again.

She closed her eyes. "Yes… yes daddy." LaLa was a Puerto Rican chick I met at the strip club a few months prior. She wasn't my lady, but she would slide through and smash every once in a while. She had the best pussy I had ever had in Florence, and I was in triple digits when it came to females.

"I'm… I'm coming Papi!" She yelled. She shook and pushed her nails into my flesh. My phone was ringing nonstop next to the bed. "Don't answer, Papi… Don't answer," LaLa begged. But I still pulled out. I knew it was Wayne by the 'Cash Money' ringtone. I had specific ringtones for everyone. "Hello," I answered.

"Four turkeys just came through the spot," Wanye said. That meant hat Rico had just dropped four kilos of crack at the spot.

"Alright, I'm coming now money." I hung up and put on my clothes.

"Santana, you just gon' leave me like that?" LaLa said, pouting.

"I got to handle some shit. I'll be back later tonight," I said. She got out of the bed and stomped to the bathroom, slamming the door. "Bitch, stop slamming doors. The fuck wrong with you?" I spat. Even though LaLa wasn't my lady, and I didn't live with her, I paid the bills. If anybody was going to slam a door, then it'd be me.

I left and got in my F-150. Before I pulled off, I called Cartel. "What's good money?" he answered.

"Yo where you at?" I asked.

"Leaving the mall."

"Meet me at the spot."

"On my way now," he said. I hung up and backed out of the yard.

- - -

#CARTEL

Somehow, we ended up at the mall. De'Asia bought me and her all kinds of shoes and clothes. She didn't rock bullshit—we went and shopped in the finest stores. She told me she liked to treat her man and she treated me with Gucci and Louis Vuitton shoes and clothes.

"Thanks baby girl," I said, getting in the car.

"Don't thank me. That's what I'm supposed to do."

"Well, do everything you 'pose to do and give yo man a kiss," I said. She leaned over the arm rest and stuck her tongue down my throat. I sucked on her tongue like it was a piece of candy. Her lip gloss tasted like strawberries.

"Damn, your lips taste good," I said.

"Yours taste better," she said. She sat down in the driver seat, then sped out of the parking lot.

"What you 'bout to do?" I asked.

"Why? You have somewhere you need to be?" she asked.

"Yeah. Santana called and said he needed me in the Projects. I told him I was coming already."

"Alright, I'll drop you off."

"Ima see you tonight though, right?" I asked.

"If you want to."

"I'll call you, then."

De'Asia dropped me off at Nina's and I rushed my bags inside. When I walked back out, De'Asia was gone. Then a text came on my phone. "Don't break my heart, Cartel." It was from De'Asia. I smiled at the text and promised her that I wouldn't, then I headed over to the spot.

Santana's F-150 was parked in front of the spot, so I figured he was inside. I walked over and did the Money Bag Gang knock. "Come in money," a voice said from the other side of the door. I opened the door and stepped in. "Lock the door behind you," Wayne said. I locked the door and then joined them at the table. "This everybody?" Wayne asked.

"Yeah, except Rico," Santana said.

"Okay, everybody know how this shit rock, put in yo' order and let's get this shit back poppin'," Wayne said, pulling out ounces of cooked crack. Santana looked over at me.

"Cartel, all the runners get whatever on consignment, just make sure you can handle what you order," Santana said.

"How much the ounces?" I asked.

"Four-hundred," Santana said.

"Nah, Rico put this one up to five-hundred. But he want me to give Cartel one on the face," Wayne said. Wayne took one ounce and slid it across the table to me. The crack was a tan color and shaped like a perfect circle.

"Alright, so this one is one the face?" I asked Wayne.

"Yeah."

"Okay, now let me buy two more." I pulled out a wad of hundreds and slid them over to Wayne.

"You know you can get them on consignment," Turk said.

"I'm good. I'll just come back when I need some more," I said. Wayne took two more ounces and slid them over to me.

"Once you move up, you'll get a monthly salary," Santana said.

"Salary?" I asked.

"Yeah. Like Trouble keeps the book and drives. He don't do transactions, but he got to get paid. So he get a salary. The only people that get paid daily are the runners," Santana explained.

"Say no more," I said, thinking things over. If I understood him correctly, then I'd rather stay a runner. The more crack I sold, the more money I got paid. Anyone else had a set pay that they received monthly.

"Let me get five money," Cam said. He was a laid-back dude, and he stayed to himself a lot. Wayne gave Cam five, then he looked at Juvie, another runner.

"Gimme five, too," Juvie said.

"Alright, don't fuck this pack up, Juvie," Santana warned.

"I got it money, chill."

"You know you on thin ice," Santana added. I didn't know what Santana was talking about, but I assumed Juvie had fucked up a few packs before. While he was getting everything in order, Trouble was hard down writing. He would look up every five seconds, then he would jot something else down.

After the orders were made, everybody went to their post. Kapo and Turk walked around the Projects on security duty. Santana was rolling up a blunt in the spot. He was the money operator, so he was waiting on the dough to start rolling in. Trouble was also in the spot. He kept the pen ready and the pad close by. Cam and Juvie sat on the couch, chopping up pieces. They were waiting on the first crackhead to knock on the door. Wayne left to put the rest of the drugs in the stash apartment, which was across the parking lot.

I ran over to Nina's apartment and rushed upstairs. I put two ounces up, and then I took the third ounce and chopped it up into twenties and grams. I wanted to see my money. I was in the middle of chopping up the ounce, when I decided to call Dough. He answered on the second ring.

"Hello," he said.

"Dough, what it do man," I said. I put the phone on speaker while I cut the crack up.

"Damn son, don't forget about me," Dough joked.

"It ain't like that. You know I been busy. The South showing mad love."

"That's good. Hey, you know the cops found Willie dead yesterday?"

"Get the fuck out of here," I said, trying my best to act surprised.

"Nobody don't know nothing Cartel. Pete mad son. You know that was his money maker."

"Yeah, I already know." I talked to Dough for a few more minutes and then I hung up. It was time to get the money.

I walked outside and made my first sale to Crackhead Pam. Pam was a real skinny lady with a good heart. "Hey nephew, hook Auntie up," she said, giving me a crumpled up twenty. I took the twenty and gave her a twenty slab. "This the same thing you had the other day?" she asked.

"Nah, that's some different shit right there."

"Everybody want that shit you had the other day. That shit been riding nephew. You know Auntie wouldn't lie to you."

"I'll try to get some of that shit again," I said.

"We'll be waiting." Pam looked at the rock in her palm again, then turned to leave. "Be safe nephew. Don't trust these people. Get you," she said as she walked back over to her apartment. Fiends were also running in and out of the spot, buying crack from Cam and Juvie. The Projects were popping, and Money Bag Gang controlled the movements.

When midnight came, I was on my second ounce. Cam and Juvie walked over to where I was posted. "Money we out. The gang 'bout to hit the club up. You rollin'?" Cam asked, pulling from a Newport.

"Nah, maybe next time," I said.

"Bet. Be on alert fam."

"I will money."

I dapped Cam and Juvie up, then they left. It was starting to get chilly, so I went inside Nina's apartment and threw on my hoodie. A minute later, I was back outside. Almost everybody else had left for the club.

"Yo' Cartel, you workin'?" Big Ben asked.

"Yeah, how much?"

"Let me get a twenty 'til tomorrow."

"I can't do that Ben. I need every penny son," I said, looking over his shoulder. There was a white truck creeping through the Projects. "Well, let me get somethin' for this fifteen," Big Ben said, pulling out fifteen ones. I took the money, then gave him a twenty rock. My eyes never left the creeping truck. "Who the fuck is that?" I asked.

Big Ben turned around and looked at the truck. "Boy, that's Kelly. You better go get that money." Ben waved his hand for her to stop.

"She good people?" I asked Ben.

"Hell yeah. Her husband a detective, so she be creeping cause she don't want him to find out."

She stopped in front of the spot, looking for Juvie or Cam. "Go 'head nephew," Big Ben said again. I walked over to the truck. She rolled down the driver side window, showing off her blonde hair and blue eyes. "You workin'?" she asked.

"Yeah, what's up?"

"Get in."

I looked inside the truck then, and back at Big Ben.

"You new?" she asked. I ignored her and walked around to the passenger side. She unlocked the door so I could get in. I got in and shut the door back. "You got somethin' for two-hundred?" she asked.

"Yeah." She gave me two crispy hundreds. I stuffed them in my pocket and gave her two grams. She looked at the two grams like she was surprised.

"You have a number?" she asked. I pulled out my phone and we exchanged numbers.

The fiends were up all night and morning, and I was up with them. I ran out of dope at three in the morning. I went inside Nina's apartment and put the money away. I was about to lay down, but I decided to call De'Asia instead. I called, not expecting an answer because it was so late, and I thought she'd be asleep. But she answered on the third ring.

"I thought you lied," she said.

"What you mean?"

"You said you would call."

"Why you still up ma?" I asked.

"I can't sleep."

"Come over so I can hold you," I said.

"Give me thirty minutes."

"Ok. Ima get in the shower," I said.

"Alright, leave the door open."

"Done."

I ended the call and unlocked the door. Then I ran upstairs to prepare for the shower. Nina still wasn't home yet. I made a mental note to call her when I woke up. I got in the shower and let the hot water cascade down my back. I washed my body with Dove soap and then rinsed it off. The shower felt good. I put more soap on a washcloth and scrubbed my body again. There was nothing like a hot shower after a long day of work selling all your drugs. I was in the shower for thirty

minutes when De'Asia eased into the shower with me. I didn't even

hear her come in the bathroom.

"You're beautiful," I said, looking at her naked body.

"I was hoping you was still in the shower," she said. I pulled her

body closer and sucked on her lips.

"Uhmmm," she moaned. My dick was standing at attention. I

pushed her back to the shower wall while sucking on her lips. The

shower water was still splashing against my back. I lifted her body up

and eased my dick inside her wetness. "Oh, shit," I said. Her insides

were warm and wet. She wrapped her legs around my waist and twirled

her hips as I shoved my dick inside and out, fast, and then slow. Her

mouth was open, but her eyes were closed. I never wanted to stop. She

palmed my head and moaned.

"Fuck," I grunted. She began to tighten her pussy muscles

around my dick. I gripped her ass cheeks and guided her up and down.

She opened her eyes and we made eye contact. I wondered what she

was thinking at that very second. She bit her bottom lip and I exploded

inside her. I would never forget that feeling. That moment in my life, I

actually felt like I was in heaven. I eased my dick back out of her, and then carried her to the bed. I laid her on her back and spread her legs. Her pussy lips were poking out. I put my head between her thighs and sucked on her clitoris. "Don't stop Cartel… don't stop."

That night, I fell in love with her. I didn't need two months or a year to fall for De'Asia. She was everything a hustler needed. She was beautiful, intelligent and she had mad class.

Chapter 6

#RICHBOY

Two weeks later, Alpo and I were trying to come up with a plan to accumulate some money. Alpo bought grams of crack here and there from some people from the East side, but we needed some real money.

"Bro, we can try that nigga Rico again," Lil-Baby said.

"Man, I ain't fuckin' with that dude. Last time we were following him was enough. That was a sign," I said. Alpo burst out laughing.

"Y'all niggas ain't never ran as fast as y'all ran that night," Alpo said.

"Nigga, you left the straps," I spat.

"Bro you still mad about them choppas?" Alpo asked.

"You damn right. Choppas don't grow on trees nigga."

"Fuck all that," Vick said. "Y'all know that nigga Zack?" he asked. Everybody knew Zack. He was over a group called the Loud Pack Pushers. The served marijuana by the pounds.

"What about Zack?" I asked.

"That's a sweet lic'. I know we can come up off that nigga," Vick said.

I thought about how much weed he'd have in his car when he served me ounces of loud. He be digging inside a whole pound bag, and still have more pounds in the backseat.

"I'm down," I said.

- - -

#Detective Shaw

"Baby, I'll be back later," I said, grabbing my car keys from the kitchen table.

"Alright, honey. I'm probably stepping out later to get me some cigarettes, but I'll be back when you get in," Kelly said.

"Yeah," I said, then I walked out the door. I got into my car and called my partner, Hicks. He answered.

"This is Detective Hicks."

"Get ready, I'm leaving my house now," I said.

"Alright, I'll be outside."

I hung up the phone and backed out of the driveway. Hicks and I had been scoping Zack Myers and his crew out for the last few days. We were trying to find somebody to take Rico's spot, since he wanted to quit moving our dope. There was too much money in the drug game to throw it all away just because a muthafucka wanted to move and start his life over. I had a mean trick up my sleeve, and I refused to let a nigger stop my money.

I picked Hicks up, then we made our way to Zack's house. He lived on the North Side, not too far from Oakland Heights Projects.

"Ima circle the block," I said, creeping past Zack's house. The sun was just going down.

"Park in the same spot," Hicks said, as he pulled out his camera. I circled the block, and then parked across the street.

"So, what all we got on these niggers?" I asked Hicks.

He turned his camera on and flipped through the photos. "To be honest Shaw, I think we're wasting our time. All this man's selling is some chump ass weed. That's not enough to make him murder Rico."

I twisted my lips up at my partner because I knew he was right. I needed something on Zack that carried a lot of time. Weed charges wouldn't make the weakest person crack. I was in deep thought when the same car that was following Rico a couple weeks ago showed up again. It crept slowly by Zack's house, as if it was also casing out the joint.

"Yo, that's the same car from the other week," Hicks said, pointing out the Crown Vic' that turned the corner.

"I know, and it looks like they were checking out Zack's house," I said. Seconds later, they turned back on the street.

"I think we got action," Hicks said.

#RICHBOY

I was loading up my 9mm as Alpo circled the block.

"His car was there, and a light was on in the house," Lil-Baby said from the backseat.

I pushed the clip inside the 9, then cracked it. "Pull up in the yard, bro," I said, ready to get the mission over with. Vick was also in the backseat. He was gripping an all-black Mac 10. Alpo bent the corner, then turned into the yard. "Let's go!" I said, jumping out of the Crown Vic' like the Feds. Alpo waited in the car while we rushed the porch. Lil-Baby and I stepped aside, and Vick kicked the front door down.

"Ahhh!" a woman screamed. I rushed inside and sent a bullet to her torso. She stumbled back, the Lil-Baby sent a bullet to her flesh, causing her to slide down the wall. I signaled for Vick to check the back rooms. He tiptoed back while I went into the kitchen. At first, it looked empty, but then I heard someone sniffing from one of the bottom cabinets.

I opened the cabinet door and found a little girl crying. She looked just like Zack. "Please... please... don't kill me," she begged, with fear in her eyes. I grabbed her by her pajama shirt and pulled her out from the cabinet. It was at that moment that I felt something sharp enter my arm. "Fuck," I grunted. The little girl snatched away from me and ran out of the kitchen.

Bam! A shot went off. Bam! Bam! Then two more shots went off. I looked at my arm, which was dripping blood. I ripped a piece of my shirt and tied my arm up. I gripped the 9mm in my other hand and walked into the living room, where the little girl was face down in a pool of her own blood.

Lil-Baby ran from the back room with two duffle bags. "Richboy, let's go!" he yelled. I thought about my blood in the kitchen. "Hold up bro," I said. I rushed back to the kitchen to try and clean up my blood so there was no D.N.A. evidence from me. "Fuck, Richboy let's go nigga!" Lil-Baby screamed again before running out the front door. I made sure all the blood was gone, then I ran from the kitchen. I jumped over the little girl's dead body before rushing out the front door.

"Drive! Drive" I shouted, getting into the backseat. Alpo pulled out of the yard and sped back to Brunson Street. That's when I realized that there were only three of us in the car.

"Where's Vick?" I asked.

"Zack killed him," Lil-Baby said.

#DETECTIVE SHAW

Hicks and I followed the Crown Vic back to Brunson Street. "Only three got out," Hicks said, snapping pictures.

"Two made it back to the car, and the driver never went in," I said.

"Where's the other guy?"

"Either he went out the back door of Zack's house or he's dead."

"I'd say the latter."

"Me too," I agreed.

It wasn't long before police cars were riding along every street in Florence. "We'll let them sleep on it. Then we'll come back probably tomorrow night," I said.

"Yeah, they ain't goin' nowhere."

Chapter 7

#CARTEL

"I'm Mary Whitewash, reporting live from Channel Fifteen News. Last night, four people were murdered here in Florence. Zack Myers was found dead inside his home, alongside Victor Boss. Also in the home were Quanya Jones, age twenty-eight, and Quaysha Myers, age seven. The police speculate the incident was a drug deal gone bad. There are no suspects at this time. If you have any information regarding the case, please contact the Florence Police Department."

I turned off the news and grabbed my phone. I had ten missed calls, and all of them were from crackheads. I wiped my eyes, and then stretched my arms.

"Cartel, you up?" Nina called from downstairs.

"Yeah!"

"I made breakfast!"

"Alright, give me a second!" I hollered back. I got out of the bed and went downstairs. "It smells good," I said, sitting down at the table.

"Thank you." Nina made me a plate and then sat in front of me. I didn't know if I wanted the sausage, eggs, or a jellied toast first. It all looked so good.

"You heard about Zack?" Nina asked, sitting across from me.

"Hell yeah. That's fucked up," I said. I stuffed my mouth with eggs and sausage.

"Man, Zack was a good dude. He never messed with nobody," Nina said, shaking her head from side to side.

"This is a cold world, Nina. Tomorrow is never promised."

"Do you ever think about death?"

"Nah. I know one day I'll die, so I just enjoy life while I'm alive. You feel me?"

"Yeah."

"How about you?" I asked between bites.

"Yeah, I think about death all the time. I try my best to live right, so I can go to heaven. But so many negative things be happening to me, I don't know if I can even believe in a God. I just feel like if a person lives right, then God suppose to make righteous things happen for you. So I just hope I go to the best place when I'm dead. Wherever that is."

I finished my plate and placed it in the sink. "Me and De'Asia going to the beach later. You want to ride along?" I asked.

"Nah, y'all go 'head."

"Santana going to," I said.

"Alright, I'll go," she said. I knew nobody liked to be the third wheel. I had to add Santana, so Nina would feel comfortable.

#RICHBOY

The murders were on every news station in South Carolina. The state was more angry about the little girl than anything. They didn't give a damn about no drug dealers, but the death of a seven-year-old made it a different story.

I was sitting at the kitchen table with Lil-Baby, Alpo and Parish. Six pounds of marijuana and one-hundred grand in cash laid out on the table in front of us. We were in the middle of splitting it.

"Man, just give me thirty-five grand and a pound," Lil-Baby said.

"Nah, everybody get thirty and we give Parish ten for using her whip," Alpo said.

"Ten grand for using the whip?" I asked, looking at Alpo crazy.

"Yeah, and we get two pounds each," Alpo added.

"I'm good, you a selfish mu…"

"Shut the fuck up Parish!" Alpo snapped, cutting her off mid-sentence. She rolled her eyes and poked her lips out. "Now look. Giving her ten bands is the least we can do bro. if Vick was here we would be giving him more than that," Alpo said, looking at me.

"Alright bro. Alright," I said as I slid Parish ten thousand. She rolled her eyes again but accepted the money. We were still splitting the money up when someone knocked on the door.

I looked at Alpo. "Who the fuck is that?"

"Nigga I don't know." Alpo looked at Parish. "Bae, go answer the door."

Parish wanted to say something but decided not to. She stood up and walked to the door. I rushed to my bedroom, just in case it was the police.

"Who is it?" Parish asked.

"Detective Shaw," a voice said from the other side of the door.

From my bedroom, I could hear Lil-Baby and Alpo fumbling with the money and the weed. "I just want to talk," Detective Shaw said. Then the door opened. My heart was racing. I couldn't go to prison. I would shoot it out and hold court on Brunson Street.

"Richboy, you might want to hear this," Detective Shaw called from the kitchen. How the fuck he know I'm in here? I thought to myself. I took a deep breath and walked out of the room. The kitchen table was empty. Alpo and Lil-Baby did a good job hiding the drugs and money. Everybody stood around the table, looking at Detective

Shaw and his partner, who held a folder in his hand. "You might want to sit down," Shaw said.

Parish sat down first, then we followed.

"Man, what the fuck you want?" I asked. I was becoming impatient.

"You shut the fuck up! And I talk!" Detective Shaw was not playing games. I looked at him like he was crazy.

"Jump muthafucka and I'll blow your shit back," Shaw said, pulling his gun from his holster. I bit my tongue and relaxed. I had to remind myself that I wasn't in a position to snap.

Detective Shaw looked at his partner, who took papers from his folder and threw them on the table. I grabbed one. It was a photo of me getting out of Parish's Crown Vic'. I looked at Shaw, then I looked at his partner.

"What the fuck," Lil-Baby said, banging on the table.

"Now y'all can either do one of two things," Shaw said.

"And what is that?" Alpo asked. Parish was sitting beside Alpo crying. She was ready to snitch at any moment.

"Y'all can work for me or do life in prison for four homicides and a home invasion."

"Work for you?" I asked.

"Yeah."

"Nigga I'm not a rat!" I snapped.

"Richboy, your mouth is going to get you in a lot of shit," Shaw said. Alpo and Lil-Baby looked at me.

"Alright, for the last decade I was giving Rico drugs for the low," Shaw said looking at me. He finally had my attention. "But he wants to retire from the game. So, he would be fucking up my money."

"So where we come in at?" Alpo asked.

"I need for y'all to bury him. Then I can start supplying y'all with the drugs."

"What about this?" Alpo asked, looking at the photos on the table.

"That goes away, until y'all niggers cross me."

The deal Shaw offered us was nothing to think about. We could get rid of the competition and get the plug all at the same time. That was killing two birds with one stone.

"And I did my research on y'all, so don't try and fuck with me," Shaw warned.

- - -

#CARTEL

De'Asia was in school. In the meantime, I drove her Lexus. I broke a rule of the gang by hustling outside of the five-block radius, but I didn't care. I had to get paid.

Santana and I were at Nina's house when Kelly called my phone.

"Hello," I answered. Kelly was the crackhead I met while I was trapping late night in the Projects.

"Cartel, you busy?" she asked.

"Nah, what's up?"

"I need you to come by."

"Alright. Give me a minute," I said, then I ended the call. "Santana, be ready when I get back," I said, standing to my feet.

"Where are you going?" he asked.

"To Effingham. But when I get back we going to the beach. De'Asia will be out of school by then."

"Ok. I'll be here money."

I got in the Lexus and headed to Effingham. I made sure I drove the speed limit. I wasn't trying to get pulled over by the police in the South. But I did have my vial for protection, so I wasn't worried.

I was crossing the Martin Luther King Bridge when it began to rain. I turned on the windshield wipers. Driving a car was like riding a bike for me. Dough and I stole cars as a hobby before we were selling dope for Willie. We would steal luxury cars and race them through the hood. I laughed at the memory as I entered Effingham, South Carolina. I had been to Kelly's house one time before, so I knew the route by heart.

I turned into the driveway and parked behind her Challenger. She lived with her husband in a two-story house. Her husband was a detective, but he was never home. He was always out working somewhere.

I put the car in park and called Kelly. "I'm outside," I said.

"Come in."

"Open the door."

I got out of the car, and it was still raining, so I rushed inside to try not to get soaked. The door was unlocked, so I opened it and stepped inside.

Kelly and her husband lived the best of the best. The inside of the house was decorated with expensive paintings and genuine leather sofas. It was similar to what I envisioned for myself in the future.

"Cartel, lock the door and come up to my bedroom," Kelly said from the stairs. She waited for me and led the way.

Kelly had blonde hair and blue eyes. She looked like she weighed about a hundred and twenty pounds, and she stood every bit of five feet four inches. She was beautiful. If I'd seen her before I had served any crack, I would've never known that she smoked. I followed her inside her room. She walked over to her dresser and grabbed four crisp hundreds.

"Give me something good, Cartel. I'm trying to relax for the entire weekend. I don't want to keep leavin' the house 'cause I know my husband might be wondering what the fuck I be doing." She laughed and passed me the four hundred dollars. I stuffed the bills in my pocket, then gave her my last four grams. I didn't mind giving Kelly five grams for four-hundred dollars. She had spent so much money that I could've just served her and been successful in my undertaking.

"That's your husband right there?" I asked, looking at a photo of them holding two rifles.

"Yeah, we were out hunting on that picture," she said, looking at the photo. It hung on the wall in a white frame. "That was a few weeks before we got married. After that, he changed." Kelly sounded sad. I could tell she needed someone to vent to.

"What do you mean he changed?" I asked.

She took a deep breath and sat down on the bed. I sat down beside her, but I left a respectful distance between us.

"Before we got married, he was very charming and respectful. He treated me like a queen, Cartel," she looked into my eyes. "We went on trips twice a year, and he made me feel like the prettiest woman on Earth," she smiled at the thought. Then the smile faded.

"But after he got the job as a detective—almost as soon as we got married—he changed. Sometimes he would stay out of the house for days at a time without answering his phone. It didn't take long before I started stressing over it." A tear fell from her eye.

"Then I started drinking with my best friend. Weeks after I had developed a drinking habit, she turned me out on crack, and I've been on it ever since." She began crying harder. I closed the gap between us and held her in my arms.

"It's alright ma… it's alright," I said. she cried on my shoulder like a baby. The moment was a very sad one, but I didn't allow myself to cry. She was still sobbing on my shoulder when Santana called me. I grabbed my phone from my pocket.

"Hello," I answered.

"Yo, Wayne want you to find Juvie and bring 'em to the spot," Santana said. Kelly left to gather herself together while I was on the phone.

"Alright, Ima stop by his spot first, and if he ain't there, then ima take a couple laps around Florence."

"Ima send you this address. It's where he might be if he not at home."

"Bet." I hung up the phone. "Yo Kelly," I said.

"Yes?" It sounded like she was in the bathroom, running the facet water.

"You good?" I asked.

"Yeah, I'm good, Cartel," she replied.

"Well, I'm out. I got something to handle," I said. I stood to my feet and walked over to the bathroom. I knocked, and then opened the door to peek inside and check on her. She was washing her face in the mirror.

"Kelly, you are a beautiful woman," I said. "Don't beat yourself up because he ain't doing the right thing. You'll know when you get tired, and once you get there, you'll be able to make the decision to leave or not," I paused for a second, then said, "If you decide to leave, he'll regret losing you. If he didn't know how special you are, then he wouldn't have married you. Remember that."

- - -

#JUVIE

I was at my baby momma's crib, smoking blunts back-to-back. I knew Wayne and Santana was looking for me. I owed the gang twenty-five hundred, and I didn't have a dime of it. My cell phone was blowing up, so I had turned it off.

My gambling habit was becoming my downfall. For some reason I thought I could go to the poker house every week and triple my money, but sometimes it didn't turn out like that. Last week was one of those times. I lost six grand in one night; that was every dollar I had to my name.

I paced the living room floor trying to come up with a plan. I couldn't keep living my life with this gambling habit. Plus, I knew Wayne was gunning for me this time. He was probably going to kill me. I had fucked up too much of his money in the past. He even told me to make sure that the last time this happened was for real the last time.

I was still roaming around the room when someone knocked on the front door. My baby momma and daughter were out, so I figured it was them returning home. I knew Santana and Wayne didn't know where I was hiding out. They were probably checking my mother's house, but I wasn't dumb enough to go there.

I went over to the front door and unlocked it, then opened it. Cartel stood in front of me. He was Gucci down to the shoes. I wanted to close the door in his face, but my heart wouldn't let me keep running.

"They sent you to kill me lil' nigga? Come on! Pop me muthafucka. I'm ready!" I said, spreading my arms. I'd given up. If they wanted to murder me, then they needed to get it over with. I was tired of running, tired of stressing, and tired of being tired. While Cartel stood in front of me, my baby momma and daughter returned home.

"Hey daddy! You staying for dinner?" my daughter asked, holding a grocery bag. I bent down until we were face-to-face.

"Baby girl, you know daddy loves you. And as long as I'm alive Ima eat every dinner with you," I promised. She smiled and wrapped her arms around my neck.

"So you and mommy are back together?" she asked. My baby momma, Cartel and I all burst out laughing.

"Yeah baby girl, we're back together," I said, looking up at her mother, who was smiling. I kissed my daughter and stood up. "Go help mommy cook, baby girl," I said. my daughter rushed inside, and her mother followed. Once they were out of earshot, I diverted my attention back to Cartel.

"Cartel look bro, I..."

He cut me off mid-sentence. "Get yo ass in the car man."

- - -

#CARTEL

On our way back to the Projects, De'Asia called me. "Hey, baby?" I answered.

"I'll be out of school in thirty minutes. We still going to the beach, right?"

"Of course."

"Alright," she said.

"I'll see you in thirty minutes," I ended the call. I turned to Juvie in an effort to change topics. "Juvie you got a good family my nigga," I said, making a left onto Church Street.

"Thanks," he mumbled.

"Everything you do should be for them Money. I'm talkin' 'bout every step you make and every breath you take should be for your daughter, son. That little girl loves you." I looked back at Juvie to make sure he was listening. A tear slid down his cheek. Juvie was in his early twenties, but I was preaching to him like I was his elder. I stopped at the stop sign and reached into my pocket. I pulled out a wad of money and counted out three grand.

"This three grand Money," I said, placing it in his palm.

"I only owe Wayne twenty-five," he said.

"I want you to take the bus to Jersey with the other five."

"Jersey?" he asked.

"Yeah, you leaving in the morning."

"What am I going to Jersey for?"

"I want you to see a friend of mine. Her name is Anna May. Ms. Anna May," I corrected myself.

Chapter 8

#RICO

Lately, something didn't feel right. It felt like someone was watching me. Every time I left my house I was watching over my shoulder. If anything looked crazy or out of place, then I. was ready to be blasting my 357 Revolver.

I sat on my bed, counting money. I was getting everything situated for when I moved. I knew De'Asia wouldn't want to leave, so I would leave her the house and plenty of money. She was welcome to pack her clothes up at any time. I would keep a room open for her.

I was still counting money when De'Asia got home from school. "Daddy you home?" she asked from downstairs.

"Yeah, baby girl, I'm up here," I said. I heard her drop her keys on the kitchen table and make her way upstairs. "I'm in the bedroom," I said, flipping through the wad of money.

"Dad, you stay counting money," she said as she stepped into my bedroom.

"That's what it's all about," I said, looking up at her.

"Why you got that gun in your lap?" she asked. I looked down at my 357. It was all chrome with a pearly-green handle. I had bought it off a crackhead when I was in Florida a while back. It was my favorite gun; I ate, slept and shit all with my 357 by my side. In fact, it was the only gun I kept in the house.

"I don't know why I got it in my lap. I meant to put it away," I said, sliding it under my pillow.

"I want me a gun like that for protection," De'Asia said. she fell in love with my 357 as soon as she first laid eyes on it.

"I told you, Ima get you a smaller gun. Ima get you something like a baby nine." She started pouting at that, and I burst out laughing. "Don't you start that shit," I said.

"But daddy!"

"Ok, baby girl. I'll give it to you on your eighteenth birthday," I said.

"You promise?"

"Yeah, I promise." She smiled from ear-to-ear when I said that. I would do anything to see that smile.

"Oh yeah. Cartel and I are heading to the beach, by the way," De'Asia said. "I just came to pack a lil' bag."

"That's what's up. Where Cartel at anyway?" I asked.

"He waiting on me downstairs."

"Tell 'em to come up here."

"Alright." De'Asia rushed out of the bedroom. A minute later, she returned with Cartel behind her. "I'll be getting my things together in my room," she said, leaving me and Cartel in the room together.

"How the South treatin' you lil' homie?" I asked.

"It couldn't be better," he said.

"You ever found that nigga Juvie?"

"Yeah. I found him hiding out at his baby momma's spot," he said.

"Did Wayne handle him like I told him?" I asked.

"Nah, he paid the money. Everything's good."

"Oh good. It was about time for him to be dealt with. He'd crossed the line too many times Cartel. He a good dude, he just got a bad gambling problem. I don't care about the gambling, just don't let your problems fuck up my paper. You feel me?"

Cartel nodded his head in agreement. "Now Ima be honest with you," I started, "I won't be around too long. I'm giving this shit up. Ima stay in touch though. In the meantime, I need you to take care of my daughter. She loves you, Cartel," I paused for a second and then continued, "Y'all remind me of me and her mother when we were your age." I smiled at the memory. "She always wanted me to get out of the game, though. I told her I would, but I had to reach my limit. I had a set number when I first got in the game, and I was determined to see it through to that number, Money. Nothing was going to stop me hitting that number. You feel me?"

"I feel you, Money," he said. Cartel and I kicked it for about another ten minutes, then he and De'Asia left for the beach. I put all of my money away, then rolled a nice, fat blunt. I puffed on the Cali bud until I could feel the buzz. Then I put it out and laid down in the bed.

I was just about asleep when I received a phone call from Detective Shaw

"Hello," I answered.

"Listen, I got my last five birds. I got them flying for five grand each. Just popped some cats from East Florence," Shaw said. Something told me to end my dealings with the Detective right then, but then he said, "This can be your last play, Rico. I'll find somebody else to move for me after this, but for now, I need the twenty-five to do some business."

"Alright. This the last play, Shaw. Then I'm done."

"Cool. Meet me at the Waffle House on fifty-two in forty-five minutes," Shaw said.

"I'll be there."

#RICHBOY

"Where the fuck this nigga at?" I asked, rubbing my AK 47 as I sat in the passenger seat of Parish's Crown Vic'.

"He'll be here any second. Just chill my nigga," Alpo said. Lil-Baby, Alpo and I sat in the Waffle House parking lot waiting on Shaw and Rico to do the transaction. Rico hadn't shown up yet; he was running late.

Five minutes later, he pulled up in his Range Rover. "Damn, I want that Range Rover dog," I said, looking at how clean Rico kept it. "I could see myself whippin' that bad boy now."

"After we get this shit out of the way, you'll be able to cop your own," Lil-Baby said.

"You ain't never lied cuz," I said. Rico got out of his car with a bag and got in the backseat of Shaw's car. "Y'all ready?" I asked, looking at Lil-Baby in the backseat.

"And you know it," Lil-Baby replied. Then I looked at Alpo. "Don't look at me like that bro. I been born ready," he said.

"That's what I'm talking about. We 'bout to put this Rich Squad shit on the map," I said. Rico got out of the car with the duffle, and then got back in his Range Rover.

"Man, whatever you do, don't forget the bricks," Lil-Baby warned. Rico backed out of the parking lot.

"Let's go," I said. Alpo eased on the gas and followed Rico down Highway Fifty-Two.

"We can get him at this light," Alpo said.

"Nah, wait 'til he make a turn," I said. "Too many cars on the highway." We followed the Range Rover as it swerved through the night. He made a left turn, and we did the same. I made sure that the doors were unlocked so that I could be prepared to jump out.

"He 'bout to stop at this light y'all," Alpo said. I grabbed my choppa and placed my finger on the trigger. The Range Rover stopped, and Alpo pulled up on the driver's side. I opened my door and sent bullets through the door of Rico's car. Lil-Baby was busting his Mac 10 from the backseat. It felt like the Fourth of July. We both lit the Range Rover up for thirty seconds straight. Over fifty bullets went through the driver's side door.

"Get to work!" Alpo shouted from the car. I stopped shooting and rushed to the Range Rover. I opened the driver's side door with my free hand. Rico was slumped over with his foot on the brakes. Lil-Baby opened the door to the backseat and grabbed the duffle bag.

"Let's go!" Alpo yelled. Before I closed the door, I took a chrome 357 Revolver from Rico's hand. The steel was cold. His 357 was no match for the AK and Mac. He never had a chance to let off even a single shot. I wiped the blood from the gun onto his designer jeans, which were also soaked in blood. Then I closed the door and jumped back into the Crown Vic'.

Alpo smashed the gas pedal and we disappeared into the night.

Chapter 9

#JUVIE

The next morning, I was off to Jersey. I still wasn't sure what I was going for. All I knew was that I was going to see a lady by the name of Ms. Anna May. Cartel gave me her address and that was it. The first thing I thought was that she may be a plug. Maybe Ms. Anna May had some bricks for the low or something. Then I thought she may be a loan shark.

On the bus, I sat beside an old man who talked to me nonstop. He had to be in his late sixties. "Son, where are you headed?" he asked me.

"I'm on my way to New Jersey."

"New Jersey…" he said as if he was recalling the memories he had there. "I used to run around in Jersey back in the eighties, when crack first hit. The crack game ripped the streets in half. It broke families up and crumbled empires."

I listened to the old man because there wasn't anything else to do on the bus. "The niggas in the streets lost their loyalty for one another," the old man continued, shaking his head from side-to-side. "A muthafucka couldn't trust his own blood brother. The only way a person would ever prosper in those streets was to be loyal to the streets and only the streets." I thought about what the man was saying. Then I thought, how do you be loyal to the streets?

Then he began again, "When I was hustling, it was me and my crew against the world. And when I say be loyal to the streets, I don't mean be loyal to everybody in the streets. I mean be loyal to everybody who was in the streets with you. Hell, fuck them niggas on the next block. Because trust me, when push came to shove, the niggas on the next block are going to say fuck you."

The old head was kicking wisdom, but it didn't mean me no good. Money Bag Gang had already revealed their true colors to me. They were strictly about money, even if it came down to lives lost. If I had shown up empty handed the day before, Wayne and Santana would've killed me on the spot. The last time I was short, they beat me until blood gushed from all parts of my face. Cartel was the only man that wasn't about the money anymore. The brother really had a heart. He did for me what a real brother would do, and I respected him for that.

I was in Washington when Wayne called my phone. "What's poppin' Money?" I answered.

"Bro where are you?" he asked.

"I'm out of town right now. I'll be back in two days, though."

"Man, Rico got killed last night. We having a meeting at the spot tonight," Wayne said.

"Rico dead?" I asked, shocked as hell.

"Yeah, but I don't want to rap on the phone. Hit me up when you get back in town."

"Say no more Money."

- - -

#SANTANA

Cartel and I got the horrible news the next morning, while we were still hanging in Myrtle Beach. I drove back to Florence while Cartel tried his best to comfort De'Asia in the backseat. The majority of the ride back was spent in silence. Nina couldn't believe it. She shed a few tears in the passenger seat. Rico was like a father to the Gang. He was very strict, but that was only when a muthafucka got out of line.

I was on the highway back to Florence when I thought about when I first met Rico. I was skipping school to sell a gram of crack I'd gotten the night before. I needed some school clothes bad. My mother wasn't working at the time, so my shoes were filled with holes and my clothes all fit too tight. I was having a hard time getting rid of the gram because everybody was going to Rico. They would walk past my apartment and straight to his. Rico would step out of his apartment and look over at me with a smirk.

I was standing all day in the Projects with the same gram. It was starting to get dark when I decided to approach him. I walked over to his apartment with anger in my heart. I felt like he was trying to play me. I knocked on the door, and a few seconds later he opened it, Coogi down to the socks. "What's good lil' homie?" he asked, looking down at me.

I looked hard up into his eyes. "I don't appreciate how you clippin' all these sales," I said, holding my chin up high. My dignity was all I had.

Rico laughed. "Lil' homie I don't owe you nothing. I been out here hustling since I was twelve. I earned this shit. You can't come outside and think you gon' grab every sale just 'cause you got rock," he paused, and then said, "When I was twelve, I had to hustle around the old heads. I came up with a strategy. I waited until they went to sleep, and then I sold until the sun rose. Because crackheads don't sleep, so while the old heads were sleeping, I was catching their sales. From that I eventually got my own clientele up."

At that second, I came up with my own strategy. Before I left, he said, "If you knock on my door again about some money, we gon' have some problems."

I snapped back into reality and laughed to myself at the memory. The wisdom he gave to me that day carried me a long way.

Instead of hustling with Rico, I hustled around him. When he slept, I was up. When he was gone, I was there.

#JUVIE

New Jersey was beautiful. It looked like everybody that moved through the city was on some important mission. They were all in a rush to their destination. I flagged down a taxicab and gave him the address. I stared out of the window as we swerved in and out of traffic. The city life was totally different from the country. I didn't see any old-school Chevies on rims. I saw more expensive cars like Bentleys and Jaguars. The females were different, even. They came in all races; Mexican, Latina and Jamaican.

I was still looking out the window when the cab driver pulled up to a house. "Sir, we are here," he said. I looked out at the street, but no one was outside. The entire street was empty. I paid the cab driver and grabbed my things.

"Thanks," I said as I got out of the cab. I walked up to the door and checked to see if I had the right address. As soon as I was certain, I knocked hesitantly. I had no idea what to expect.

"Come in," a raspy voice said from the other side of the door. I twisted the knob and opened the door. "Come in and have a seat. Ali told me you would be coming." I dropped my things by the front door and made my way towards the table in the center of the room.

"Who is Ali?" I asked.

"Well, that is Cartel's father," an older woman said as she slowly emerged from the corner of the room.

"Oh."

The woman looked into my eyes, then she said, "Jalen Frost."

I was completely stunned. Jalen Frost was my father. I wasn't sure how she knew his name, but I didn't bother to ask. I trusted Cartel, and I believe he sent me here for a reason. I looked at the woman, I could tell there was something special about her.

"Jalen Frost is watching over you, son. But his spirit is not at peace. He is worried about you," she paused and slid me a folded sheet of paper. "Don't open this until you are ready to live. What's on the paper is in line with your D.N.A." Ms. Anna May then slid me a wooden bracelet. "Wear this on your left wrist. It will protect you from evil spirits. Don't lose it," she said. I grabbed the bracelet and placed it on my left wrist.

"Can I ask you a question?" I asked her.

"Sure," she replied.

"Why isn't my father's spirit at peace?"

"Well, you are not at. Peace. Once you are living in peace, then he will, too. It seems as though you are riddled with some sort of addiction."

"Addiction?" I asked.

She stared into my eyes without blinking. "Yes. You... hmm... have a... hmm... gambling addiction, son."

My heart sped up. "Yeah. Yeah, I do, and I'm working on it," I stumbled over my words.

"Well, he's not very happy with it. Especially because gambling is what caused his own demise." Ms. Anna May wasn't wrong. My father was shot by a mob boss that he owed from a gambling debt. The same boss was murdered a week later by my uncle Larry, who sits on death row now.

"But don't worry," she said. "Follow your D.N.A." She nodded to the folded paper I held in my hand. "It will guide you, and then your father's spirit will be at peace."

Chapter 10

#PARISH

Alpo and Richboy were putting me in a crazy situation. Somehow, they thought it was a good idea for me to go to Rico's funeral. They said that my appearance would say a lot. As much as I didn't want to go, they left me with no options. I got dressed just in time to ride with De'Asia and Cartel in the limo. I could tell De'Asia missed me being around, especially now that times are so hard. Whenever she wasn't hugging on Cartel, she was cuddled up on my shoulder.

Inside the church, I sat in the front row with De'Asia and Cartel. The funeral was filled with dope boys and gangsters from all over Florence. They all showed up to show Rico the respect he deserved. Everybody was dressed in black. I wore my black dress, black heels and my black Ray Bands. I didn't want anyone to see my eyes. Cartel sported an expensive suit, with a pair of snake-skin Stacy Adams and his money green bandana wrapped around his head.

Cartel was real observant; he paid close attention to the crowd, but he didn't say much. To be honest, he made me very nervous. I wanted to know what he was thinking. Did he know? I thought to myself. Of course he didn't know. If he had known, I wouldn't have made it to the funeral.

I was stressed out listening to the preacher, so I stepped outside and grabbed a Newport from a man who was also attending the funeral. I puffed the cigarette like it was the last one on earth. I was still puffing when Cartel stepped outside. He stared at the dark clouds above and inhaled.

"You alright?" he asked. I flicked the cigarette and stepped on it.

"Huh?" I asked, not sure if he was talking to me.

"Are you alright?" he asked again, stepping closer to me. "De'Asia wanted me to check on you. She said Rico was like an uncle to you." The words punched me right in the heart.

"Yes... Rico was like... my uncle," I stuttered. Cartel came closer and wrapped his arms around me. I could feel his gun on his hip.

"I didn't know Rico that long," Cartel said softly. "But I know he was an amazing guy. He helped a lot of people, so it's only right that a lot of people feel hurt right now. But I know he'd want y'all to be strong. Take his death as motivation instead of pain, because I know for a fact that he wouldn't want to see De'Asia hurt like this. And knowing you is like De'Asia sister, he wouldn't want you in pain either."

Tears flooded from my eyes as I thought about Rico. He was like the father I never had. But I was so in love with Alpo that I was willing to cross all lines to feel his love. Even if all that meant hurting myself in the process. Cartel held me until I stopped crying.

"Do y'all know who did it?" I asked.

"Nah, but we'll find out. In the meantime, I need you and De'Asia to be there for one another."

"Alright."

- - -

#RICHBOY

The bloody red Range Rover, fresh off the lot, said so much about how I felt. I swerved through traffic, heading back to Brunson Street. Young Jeezy's voice blasted through the speakers as I bent the corners entering North Florence. I rolled the windows down so muthafuckas could see me.

I turned onto Brunson Street with my arm out the window. All eyes were on me. I pulled into the yard and parked. Alpo and Lil-Baby had fiends running in and out like we were running some type of fast-food restaurant. Life couldn't be better on Brunson Street. Everybody looked like they had risen from the dead.

"Richboy, you straight?" a fiend asked. I killed my engine and stepped out of the truck.

"I ain't even pull my shit out yet unc'. Go holla at Alpo," I said.

"Alright." The fiend rushed into the house. I was walking behind him when I noticed two twin brothers looking at my Range Rover. "Y'all niggas like that, huh?" I asked.

"Hell yeah," they both said in unison. The two couldn't have been older than sixteen.

"How old y'all is?" I asked.

"We turnt sixteen today," one said.

"Oh, word. What y'all doin' for it?"

They both dropped their heads. "Nancy ain't trying to throw us a party," the other said.

"Nancy y'all mother?" I asked.

"Yeah." Nancy was an older woman who ran up and down Brunson Street smoking crack. I pulled out a wad of hundreds. I peeled a couple bills off the top and handed it to them.

"Damn, thanks Richboy!" They both smiled from ear to ear.

"Happy birthday. Y'all go grab some outfits for the party tonight at Peter Rabbit," I said.

"Say no more." They dapped me up.

"I forgot y'all name," I said,

"Deon and Keon, but everybody called us Deebo and Kilo."

"You're Kilo?" I asked, pointing to the smaller one.

"Yeah," he said. The kid was just slightly smaller than his brother, but other than size, they were identical.

"Bet. Deebo and Kilo," I said, making sure I had the names right.

"Yup," Kilo said.

I dapped them up and turned to leave. "Richboy," Deebo called. I turned back around. "What's with that Rich Squad shit?" he asked. I thought about it for a second. We would need help with the bricks Shaw was bringing. I could easily sell them ounces for five hundred and still profit. It was a win-win situation.

"Welcome to the Squad, twins," I said. They both smiled like they had signed a deal with Bad Boyz Records.

- - -

#ALPO

Peter Rabbit was a small store on Brunson Street. All the fiends and dope boys chilled at the store to watch football or basketball games. Some people just stopped by to get away from their wives for a couple hours.

The store was one of the only places a crack head could go without being judged. There was much love in the store, and tonight was Deebo and Kilo's birthday party. A lot of people were inside the store, but the majority of the crowd was out in the parking lot.

Lil-Baby and I sat on the hood of his new Impala, smoking a kush-filled blunt. "Damn, it feels good tonight cuz," Lil-Baby said, blowing the weed smoke into the night.

"Yeah, it do feel good," I agreed. The party was full of dope boys, hoodrats, divas, crack heads and jack boys who were all either from Brunson Street, or just a few blocks down the road. The liquor and weed were free, but the crack was still for sale.

"Yo Jemilla! Bring me a plate!" I yelled. Jemilla was a Northside whore. Everybody and their daddy knew what the pussy was like. But she still had mad respect on the block. She was known to bust a bitch head. She was the woman we called when our woman got out of line, and we didn't want to be the one to slap her. Five minutes later, Jemilla delivered a healthy plate. "Thanks," I said.

Lil-Baby stared at her ass as she walked away. "Man, I would've wifed Jemilla if she wasn't a thot," he said. Jemilla was beautiful. She was a red bone, with nice lips. She stood at about five foot nine, and she had a body like a stripper. Her hair was long and curly like she was mixed with another race.

I bit into a piece of chicken. "Boy you better grab a plate before the shit be gone," I warned Lil-Baby.

"I ain't hungry right now," he said.

"That's why you're small now," I said. Lil-Baby weighed about one hundred and ten pounds and was only five foot six. He could stand to get bigger, especially considering the game we were in.

I was still eating when I noticed my baby mother getting out of her mother's minivan. She and I had a three-year-old son together; she got pregnant when I was fifteen. "Sonya!" I yelled, waving her over. She walked over looking like Beyonce. My dick stood up instantly. "I'll be in the store if you need me," Lil-Baby said.

"Alright," I said, barely hearing what he said. He slid off the hood and walked inside Peter Rabbit. "You look beautiful," I said to Sonya. She rolled her eyes and leaned on the hood.

"What you want Allen," she said, calling me by my government name. She only called me that whenever she was upset. I laughed and chewed on my last piece of chicken. "I missed you," I said.

"Boy whatever. Where yo bitch at?" she asked.

"Who?" I asked, knowing she was talking about Parish.

"Allen, I don't have time for the games."

"Baby listen. It ain't even like that with me and Parish. Every second I'm with her I'm still thinking of you," I said, putting my plate to the side. She blushed and poked her lips out. I stood up. "I love you, Sonya. Can't no woman take your place," I said.

"I love you too, Alpo."

That night I turned my phone off and spent the night with Sonya and my son, Junior. She lived at her mother's house, just a few blocks from Brunson Street. That night I promised her I would buy her a car and a house. I didn't want her living with her mother anymore.

"Promise me something else," Sonya said.

"What?" I asked.

"I want you to promise that you won't leave us." I looked and Sonya and thought about junior. "I promise," I said.

For some reason, I felt like I was doing the right thing as a man. Every son needed their father. I couldn't leave my son out in this cold world to survive on his own. It was time for me to step up and be the father I knew I could be. I didn't want to be one of those men that had two and three baby mothers, all on child support, just struggling to get by.

I also had to take advantage of the opportunity Shaw gave us. There was no telling how long he would supply us with the drugs. When all was said and done, he was still part of the police, and the police could never be trusted.

Chapter 11

#CARTEL

Wayne called a meeting two days after the funeral. Everybody showed up except Trouble and Turk. They were both off handling some important business for Wayne, so he continued the meeting without them.

"Well, y'all already know that everybody moved up one rank," Wayne started. "But we aren't doing the driver or bookkeeper no more. I'm the Head Nigga in charge, Santana is the Captain, Trouble is the Lieutenant, Kapo is Sergeant, Turk and Cam are Enforcers, and Juvie and Cartel are Runners." Wayne looked at everyone to make sure they understood.

"But we got one problem," Wayne said.

"What's that/" Santana asked.

"Rico never told me who the connect was."

"Get the fuck out of here," Cam said.

"For real. I guess we never thought shit would pop off like this," Wayne added.

"So we can't get no dope right now?" I asked.

"Nah. Not unless we go cop from somebody around town. But if we do that, we still ain't getting' no deal. They goin' to tax us like regular muthafuckas," Wayne said. I still had six ounces, but that shit would be gone by the end of the week.

"I probably can go cop something from them boys off Brunson Street," Santana said.

"Rich Squad?" Wayne asked.

"Yeah, I heard them boys plugged in on some work."

"Who they plugged in with?" Kapo asked.

"I don't know," Santana said.

"Alright, fuck who the plug. Go see what the ticket is. If they talking right, we can cop from them until we find a new plug," Wayne said.

"Bet. Ride wit' me Cartel," Santana said, walking towards the door. I stood up and followed him out the door.

We both got into his F-150. He drove out of the parking lot as he sparked a cigarette. "That's crazy Wayne don't know who the plug is," I said, looking at Santana.

"Yeah, Rico was real low-key," Santana said. He made a right turn, and then a sharp left onto Brunson Street. Crack heads were walking up and down the street like zombies. The scene reminded me of that Frank Lucas movie. Santana slowed down and turned into a yard with two men sitting on the front porch. Santana parked beside a red Range Rover; it reminded me of Rico's old car. We got out of the truck and walked up onto the porch.

"Richboy and Lil-Baby, this my fam Cartel. Cartel, Richboy and Lil-Baby," Santana said, introducing us. We nodded our heads to acknowledge one another.

"What brings y'all over to the block?" Richboy asked.

"Well, I know y'all heard about Rico," Santana said, between puffs of his Newport.

"And?" Lil-Baby asked.

"The Gang need some work," Santana said. Richboy and Lil-Baby looked at each other, then Richboy averted his attention back to Santana.

"That seems like a personal problem," Richboy said.

"Damn, you gon' play the game like that?"

"Santana, it ain't no beef between the Squad and the Gang. But please don't act like it's all love."

"Say no more Rich." Santana turned to leave, and I followed. I didn't know Richboy, but something seemed funny about him. I didn't like his character.

- - -

#DE'ASIA

Parish and I left the mall before it got dark. I had spent a grand on shoes for Cartel and I. Although my father left me the house and a little over a hundred grand, I knew I needed to slow down on my spending habits. A hundred grand wouldn't last too long if I continued spending the way I was. Especially with no means of income.

I turned onto Irby Street and stopped at the light. "Alpo ass ain't answered the damn phone in two fucking days!" Parish fussed from the passenger seat.

"I don't know why you follow up with that boy," I said.

"Don't start De'."

"Alright." She put her phone away with an attitude.

"Go to Brunson Street real fast," she said.

"Parish, I ain't 'bout to be chasing no nigga down."

"Girl I'm not about to chase Alpo down. I just want to see if he's over there." I rolled my eyes and made a right turn.

"I'm not staying over here too long Parish," I warned. I turned onto Brunson Street slowly, then turned into Alpo and Richboy's yard.

"I'm coming right back," Parish said, pushing the door open. Before she could get out, a brand-new Charger swerved into the yard. "What the fuck!" Parish said, looking at the Charger. "Bitch got me fucked up!" I turned my head and saw Parish rushing to the passenger side. I didn't realize what was going on until I saw Parish pull Alpo's baby mother form the car. Alpo jumped out of the driver's seat.

"Parish! Chill the fuck out yo!" he yelled, rushing to his baby momma's aid. Parish had a fistful of her hair in one hand and was pounding her with the other.

"Beat her ass Parish!" I shouted out the car window. Alpo grabbed Parish, pulling her by her shirt. I backed out of the yard so I could drive off when Parish got in the car.

"Let me go mu'fucka!" Parish spat, biting Alpo's hand.

"Ah fuck!" he said, holding his hand with the other. By this point, Richboy and Lil-Baby were on the front porch.

"Parish come on!" I yelled. She was running back to the car when Alpo's baby mother caught her from behind. Parish stumbled forward and fell to the concrete. It wasn't long before Alpo's baby mother was stomping Parish's face.

"Oh hell nah!" I said, watching the blood squirt onto the ground. Alpo rushed over and slung his baby mother off Parish. She stumbled and tripped, somehow landing in front of my car. She struggled to her feet. Slowly, we made eye contact as she stood up. I don't remember thinking. All I know is that my car crashed into her. *Eerrkkk!* I smashed on the brakes, and she rolled off the hood of the car.

"Sonya!" Alpo yelled, rushing over to her body. I went numb, but my heart was beating a hundred miles per hour.

"Bitch go! Go!" Parish said, getting into the passenger seat. Blood was dripping from her lip and nose. I looked back at Alpo holding Sonya in his arms. Then shots went off. *Blaw! Blaw!* I stepped on the gas, and we made a fast right at the stop sign.

"Oh my God... oh my God," Parish was saying. Looking back. I'd never been so scared in my life. I didn't know where to go or what to do. "You think she dead?" I asked.

"Fuck... I don't know," Parish took off her shirt and wiped her nose. "I think my fucking nose broke," she said.

- - -

#CRACK HEAD NANCY

I watched as the car crushed that girl's bones. It was a horrible sight to see. I prayed she made it out alive, but it didn't look like she would. Alpo held her until the ambulance came. She was rushed to the hospital, and everybody followed in their cars.

"Ma, you coming?" Deebo asked.

"No, you go 'head. I'll be at home," I said. Deebo got in the Range Rover with Richboy and Lil-Baby. Before I knew it, I was standing alone in the yard. I was about to walk home when I remembered that I came out to grab me something to smoke. I stopped and looked back at the house. I wasn't sure if anyone stayed back or not. I walked up onto the porch and noticed that the front door was ajar.

"Hello? Anyone in here?" I asked, pushing the door open. No one answered. "Hellooo!" I doubled checked, but I still didn't get an answer. I looked back to see if anyone was looking, and then I crept inside.

My adrenaline was rushing. I knew if I got caught, I would be killed. There was no doubt about that. I ran into the bedroom and grabbed anything I could find. I found a stack of cash under the pillow. I stuffed it in my pocket and continued. I knew I had to hurry. I lifted the mattress up and saw a gun. It was all chrome with a green pearl handle.

#JUVIE

Santana turned into the Projects listening to a Lil' Boosie track.

I was serving a crack fiend a twenty rock outside the spot. "Thanks

nephew," the crack head said, putting the rock in a small bag. Nephew

was the name every crack head called a dope boy in Florence. If the

dope boy didn't use the crack fiend's name, we called them unc' or

auntie.

"You good unc'," I said. Santana and Cartel got out of the

Range Rover and walked over. "What's the ticket?" I asked.

"Them niggas trippin'. We got to go roll on somebody else,"

Santana said.

"Them niggas always been funny on Brunson," I said.

"Yeah. Wayne still inside?" Santana asked.

"Yeah, they waiting on you." Santana walked inside the spot,

but Cartel and I stayed outside.

"What's good fam?" Cartel asked me. I hadn't had a chance to

tell him about the trip to Jersey. I'd been so busy trying to stay focused.

"Everything is love my nigga. I meant to thank you for sending me up there to Jersey. That shit was blessing Money."

"Yeah. Ms. Anna May is the truth bro. Make sure you stay on track too because it'll make you live better," he said.

"I already know." I adjusted the wooden bracelet on my wrist. I didn't tell Cartel about my D.N.A., but the paper Ms. Anna May gave me said a few things about it. Gambling, drugs and alcohol didn't agree with my D.N.A., and any one of the three could easily bring me down. It also said that my D.N.A. normally made bad choices because of anxiety. A mentor or some type of leadership from a positive-minded person would help me with my decision making. The last line on the paper said I was a sybarite, who was anyone fond of luxury and pleasure. But I found luxury and pleasure in the wrong things. I memorized the paper and to my best to stay conscious of it always. Cartel's phone went off then, interrupting my train of thought.

"Hello," he answered. "Yeah, I'm in the Projects… ok." He ended the call.

"You 'bout to ride out?" I asked.

"Nah, someone want some work." A second later, a white lady pulled up and Cartel got in the car. While he was making his transaction, crack head Nancy walked up.

"Nephew, you got some work?" she asked, looking over her shoulder.

"Yeah, what you need?" I asked.

"Give me something good for a hundred." She handed me a crispy hundred-dollar bill. I dug in my pocket and pulled out a bag of chopped up crack. I picked out a few rocks and placed them in her palm. "Damn Nephew I know you can do better than that," she said, fumbling with the rocks.

"Auntie don't do that," I said. I knew I had given her more than her money's worth. She was just trying to get extra like the typical crack head. Cartel got out of the car and walked over.

"Well, what you'll give me for this?" Nancy asked, pulling out a chrome 357 with a green pearl handle.

"That muthafucka is nice," Cartel said, taking it out of her hand. "How much you want for this?" he asked. I didn't interrupt the transaction because I wasn't trying to spend any money. I had to stay focused.

"Just give me something Nephew," Nancy said, looking over her shoulder again. Cartel tucked the 357 and gave her a gram of crack. "That's what I'm talking 'bout Nephew!" Nancy said, smiling. "Oh, and y'all heard about that shit on Brunson Street?" she asked.

"No, what happened?" I asked.

"Two or three muthafuckas was fighting like cats and dogs. One girl roll over somebody, and the other people shot the car up. I think the person that got run over is dead, but I prayed for her though."

"They wildin' in the North," I said, shaking my head from side to side.

#DE'ASIA

I dropped Parish off at home and went straight to my house. I was still shaken up. I rushed into the house and turned the news on. My face was the first thing I saw. I was wanted for attempted murder, which meant Sonya was still alive. I turned the T.V. off and began to pace the floor.

After a while, I decided to call Cartel. He answered. "Baby where are you... Please come to my house A.S.A.P. Just come Cartel," I said, shaking. He said he was on his way. I dropped my cell phone on the floor and went into the kitchen. I made myself a glass of wine to help me calm down. Before I knew it, I was on my second glass. Cartel rushed in the house twenty minutes later.

"De'Asia what's wrong?" he asked. I was so happy to see him. I wrapped my arms around his body and cried into his chest.

"They... they're looking... looking for me," I mumbled into his chest.

"Calm down baby. Who looking for you?" Cartel backed up and lifted up his shirt. He took a gun from his hip and placed it on the kitchen table. My heart dropped and all my energy left my body. I fell to my knees. "Baby, get up," Cartel said.

"Florence Police Department!" the Police shouted as they kicked open the door. They rushed inside and arrested me. They had to carry me to the police car because my body wouldn't move. I couldn't even tell Cartel that I knew he murdered my father; I didn't have the energy to. The only image I saw was the night my father sat on the bed with the same gun Cartel placed on the table. I know he had it with him the night he was murdered.

The ride to the County Jail was like a nightmare. So much was going through my head, I didn't know where to start or even put it in order. There was enough on my mind to drive any woman insane. We arrived to the County Jail about an hour later. The Police led me inside with my hands cuffed behind my back.

"You can take the cuffs off of her," a Correctional Officer said. The Officer was an older black lady. She was no older than thirty. The other officer uncuffed me. "Come over here De'Asia," the Correctional Officer ordered, walking to a small room. I followed behind her, wondering how she knew my name. I walked inside the room and she closed the door.

"I'm 'pose to search you, but you know I ain't with that shit," she said. I could tell she was from the Ghetto. She twisted her neck with every word. "Just chill with me so they'll think I'm searching," she added.

"Al-... alright," I stuttered.

"Wayne and Santana comin' to bond you out?" she asked.

"Do I know you?" I asked.

"Girl, I'm Shelly. I used to talk to Wayne a couple years back."

"Oh," I said. I still didn't know who she was. Wayne had so many women that it was impossible to keep up with the names and faces, but I didn't tell her that. "Yeah, Wayne should come get me," I said.

"Well, you won't see the Judge until tomorrow morning." I dropped my head. "De'Asia everything will be alright. I got to have faith that it will though," she said. Tears fell from my eyes and dropped to the jail floor.

"Pick your head up De'Asia." Shelly put her finger on my chin and lifted my face up. Then she said, "I don't know what happened on Brunson Street. It ain't my business. But I do know you is a good girl who just got into a bad situation. Your father was a strong black man, so I know the strength is in you. You just got to pull is out." Shelly

preached for another minute and then dressed me in a bright orange

jumpsuit.

"You would usually stay up front until your bond hearing, but

something is wrong with the cells so I'm putting you in the back." She

gave me a pair of orange slippers to match my jumpsuit. "You know

Nova?" Shelly asked.

The name sounded familiar, but I couldn't put a face with it.

"The name rings a bell," I said.

"Nova's my cousin. She's from Wilson Road." Wilson Road

was a spot in North Florence, not too far from the Projects. That area

wasn't getting money like Rich Squad or Money Bag Gang, but they

were hustling a couple grams of crack out there. "Ima put you in a cell

with her. She's good people," Shelly said.

I nodded my head and followed her out of the room. The

Correctional Officers booked me, took my photo and got my

fingerprints. Then another Officer took me to the back. The jumpsuit

was baggy, so I rolled the pant legs up a little bit. I followed the Officer

until we got to a door that had 'E-Pod' plastered on the front in white bold letters. The door slid open slowly. Then I stepped inside the pod, and it slammed back, making a loud noise.

Orange jumpsuits were everywhere. The pod had a top and bottom floor. When the door slammed, all eyes were on me like I was some type of fresh meat. I looked around and noticed one familiar face out of the crowd. She looked just like the rapper Da Brat. She approached me with a book in her hand.

"De'Asia, I'm Nova," she said.

"Yeah, your face looked familiar," I said.

"I used to cop grams from your pops sometimes. Then he started sending me to the lil' runners when he got too big to sell grams." We both laughed. "Rico said, 'Nova I don't sell peanuts, but Juvie might sell you somethin' baby girl.'" Nova imitated my father down to the way he spoke. I laughed again; it was the first time I had laughed in a while.

"Yeah, that's my daddy," I said. From the outside, Nova looked like a gangster. She had tattoos all over her body, including a teardrop on her face. Every tooth in her mouth was gold, and she wore her hair neatly corn rolled down the back.

"You're my cellmate. We in one-eighty-seven," she said, pointing to a cell on the bottom floor. "Everything I got is yours De'Asia. I know you'll be gone tomorrow, but in the meantime, kick back and relax," Nova said. I went to the cell and got myself together. It was a small cell with a bunk bed and a sink that was connected to the toilet. Nova brought me two sheets and a blanket to make my bed.

"You want the bottom bunk? It be hell climbing up on top," Nova said. The bunk bed didn't have steps for a person to climb on, so I would have to jump up on it and jump back down. "Yeah, let's switch," I said. I stepped back while Nova moved our beds around.

"Lock down!" the Correctional Officer shouted outside the door.

"What's she talking about?" I asked.

"She's locking our doors for the tonight," Nova said. The Correctional Officer locked all the cell doors and then left the pod.

"They'll open the doors back in the morning though," Nova said, straightening my bunk.

"How long you been in here?" I asked.

"Two years. I suppose to go to trial soon."

"Damn, what you do?

"You don't remember Calvin Little from the East Side?" Nova asked, jumping onto the top bunk.

"Calvin Little? He sold the clothes and shoes out his trunk?" I asked.

"Yeah. He got murdered a couple years back and my name got caught in the mix. But I pray I beat 'em in trial."

"When you go to trial?" I asked.

"My lawyer try'na get me in there sometime next year."

"That's what's up." I kicked my slippers off and sat on the bed.

"De'Asia, did y'all ever find out who rolled on your pops?" Nova asked. The question caught me off guard. I took a deep breath. "Nah. But I think I know who did it," I said.

"Yeah?" Nova looked down at me.

"Yeah. See my father had this gun. But it was like a unique gun, Nova. Nobody else got this gun in this color. At least I never seen it."

"How it looked?" Nova asked.

"The shit was like chrome, with a pearl green handle." I paused for a second, then said, "My father had it the night he died. I seen it with him before Cartel and I went to..." I stopped mid-sentence.

"What?" Nova asked.

"Cartel had my pops gun today. But he was at the beach when my father died," I said.

"Who is Cartel?"

"That's my boyfriend." I scratched my head, trying to connect the dots. It was impossible for Cartel to kill my father while we were at the beach.

"You think someone might've gave him the gun?" Nova asked.

"Cartel don't know nobody down here but Money Bag Gang. He just moved from Jersey." There was a long pause, then Nova said, "You think somebody in the Gang could've done it?"

"I don't know. Why would they want to kill my father?" I asked.

"Money, a woman, hate, position. I don't know but you do know your boyfriend had the gun." One word stuck out to me when Nova finished her sentence: position. "Maybe someone wanted his rank," I said.

"Yeah, muthafuckas real dirty, De'Asia. I don't put it past them niggas. 'Cause who else got the guts to kill Rico? A bitch would kill their mother before they fucked with Rico. That shit don't sound right."

"That's probably why Cartel and Santana took me and Nina to the beach. They wanted me to be gone," I said.

"Or that was just their way to make an alibi," Nova added. Everything pointed to Money Bag Gang. There was no way around Cartel having my father's gun. I laid down in the bunk, trying to rest my soul. But I couldn't relax, so I stayed up staring at the wall. I had too much on my mind to sleep.

Chapter 12

#RICHBOY

The twins and I were in the house when I noticed that my gun and money were gone. "Somebody must've came in while we were at the hospital," Kilo said.

I joined Kilo and Deebo at the table. "Whoever it was had to be a crackhead because they didn't even search good. I got a quarter brick in the kitchen cabinet," I said.

"Crackhead or not, they still need to be dealt with," Deebo said, twisting up his lip.

"You want us to go out there and come up with a muthafucka?" Kilo asked. I smiled at my two goons. They were ready for some action.

"Nah, save that energy for something serious. We need to get this paper right now," I said. I was thinking about calling to check on Alpo when Detective Shaw called my phone. "What's up?" I answered.

"Y'all want to get paid or fight over some bitches?" Shaw asked.

"Man, what's up? You got something for me or not?" I asked, ignoring his smart-ass mouth. He was a slick talking ass white man.

"You on Brunson?" he asked.

"Yeah."

"I'll be there in ten minutes."

"Bet." I ended the call. "Shaw coming through. I hope he got a couple bricks," I said.

"I told you my people from the East want a half block," Deebo said.

"I only got a quarter right now. Unless you want to see what Shaw got."

"Yeah, I'll wait," he said. I called Lil-Baby and told him Shaw was coming through. He said he was in Hartsville, but he would be back in town later that night. I thought again about calling my brother Alpo, but I knew he wanted to stay with Sonya in the hospital. She was in bad shape and needed some type of support.

Detective Shaw and his partner Hicks arrived in a white Charger. They both got out of the car with book bags. Deebo opened the door for them and locked it behind them.

"Rich, we need to find a better place to meet next time," Shaw said, giving me the book bag.

"You scared to come through the hood at night nigga?" I asked, unzipping the bag.

"No. A white man like myself just don't look right coming to a neighborhood like this." Shaw sat down at the table. Detective Hicks decided to stand.

"White men like yourself come buy crack from neighborhoods like this all the time," I shot back, looking at the marijuana inside the bag. "What Ima do with some weed?" I asked.

"Hicks got a brick of coke in the other bag. We hit some low life muthafuckas today," Shaw said. I passed the marijuana to Deebo. "I can't do nothing with that," I said, taking the bag from Hicks. I unzipped the bag and pulled the coke out. "Now, I can do somethin' with this," I said.

"Give me five grand for the dope," Shaw said. Deebo passed the pound of marijuana to Kilo. He looked at it for a second. "How much you want for the bud?" Kilo asked.

"I don't know, just give me a grand," Shaw said. Kilo pulled out a grand and placed it in front of Shaw. I counted out five grand and the deal was done. "And y'all keep the noise down over here. We can't get money if the whole block is on the damn news," Shaw said as soon as he stood to his feet.

"We got that under control. You just worry about doing a bigger bust next time," I said. Shaw rolled his eyes like a bitch and walked out the door, followed by his partner Hicks.

"Damn, I hate that cracker!" Deebo spat once they were out of earshot.

"I love 'em. He just sold me three pounds of damn loud for a thousand. It can't get no better than that!" Kilo smiled, laying the three pounds on the table.

- - -

#ALPO

My son was at his grandmother's house while I sat at the hospital with his mother. I didn't want him to see her with tubes down her throat, hooked up to all these machines. Nobody would want to see their mother in that condition.

Parish kept calling my phone, but I kept declining her calls. The doctor entered the room around ten o'clock that night and told me I had to leave, but I could return the next day. I kissed Sonya on the forehead before I left.

On my way out of the hospital, Lil-Baby called my cell phone. "Talk to me lil' bro," I answered.

"How you feeling my nigga?" he asked.

"I'm alright. The doctor said she got some broken bones, but nothing life-threatening."

"That's good. You spending the night up there?"

"No, they told me I could come back tomorrow." I got into my car and drove out of the parking lot.

"Well, I'm about to hit the club up. You can roll if you want," Lil-Baby said. I didn't want to go to the club, but I knew a drink would clear my head. "Give me about an hour fam. I'll meet you in the hood," I said.

"Got you my nigga." We hung up and I drove home. Sonya and I moved into an apartment on the South Side. It was in a better community than Brunson Street. I didn't have to worry about no bullshit going on.

When I got home, I got in the shower. I took a twenty-minute shower, then got dressed in a black and white L.R.G outfit. I completed the look with a pair of white Air Forces and a black and white Atlanta snap-back hat. I double-checked myself in the mirror before I left the house.

I was getting in the car when I noticed a black Honda with tinted windows creeping by. It drove by slowly, then made a left at the corner. Something was very suspicious about the car. It gave me a bad vibe.

#PARISH

I followed Alpo from the hospital to his new apartment in South Florence. He didn't notice me because I drove my aunt's black Honda. It looked like he was leaving, so I left. I decided to give him some space for a while.

In the meantime, I went to Walmart and grabbed three small cameras for a house. I got back in the car and sparked a cigarette. I smoked it as I drove back to Alpo's place. I smoked the entire cigarette, then sparked another.

I was halfway done with my second cigarette when I got back to Alpo's place. I finished it, then flicked it out the window. Before I got out of my car, I connected the cameras to my phone. I got out of the car and locked the door back. The night air was December cold. I looked around the apartment complex to make sure no one was looking, then I rushed to the apartment and picked the lock with my I.D. card. I pushed the door open. The lovely smell of my man's cologne invaded my nose.

"Damn, my baby smell good," I said to myself. I closed the door behind me and walked through the apartment. I could tell they weren't done moving in. The only had one small sofa in the living room, which was beside a 50-inch T.V. I walked down the hall until I reached the bedroom. I opened the door.

The sight of Alpo's son's toys made my stomach turn. I hated his son with all my heart. Whenever I saw Alpo's son, he reminded me of what Alpo and Sonya used to have. His son was also the reason he kept going back to Sonya. I knew if I could get rid of their son, their relationship would crumble.

I stepped over a basketball in the child room and placed a camera where no one would notice it. Next, I went to the master bedroom and the bathroom so I could place the other cameras. I walked around the apartment for a few more minutes, then I left.

Once outside, I called Alpo's cell phone. It went straight to voicemail, so I left a message:

"Hey love. I know you need some time to yourself. And I understand. I want you to know I'm not mad at you. I'm mad at myself for not being who I need to be. Which is a Queen to my King. But when you are ready to start over, I will be here. And I will be that Queen that you need for me to be. I will go get a job if you want me to.

I will do more cleaning as well. Just teach me Allen, and I promise I will do it. I love you baby."

I hung up and got in the car. I sparked a Newport and drove to my aunt's house. She lived in the country by herself. I put the cigarette out when I arrived. I rushed into the house and went upstairs. I locked the bedroom door so no one could come inside, then I jumped on the bed to wait for my man to come home.

He got home at four in the morning. He took off his clothes and got into the shower. My pussy was becoming moist. He stayed in the shower for ten minutes, then he got out. The sight of his dick hanging made my pussy throb. I took off my pants and thong. He entered the bedroom and began rubbing lotion over his body. I slipped my fingers in my wetness and stroked my clit. "Fuck!" It felt so good. I looked at Alpo's nine-inch dick and imagined it penetrating my insides.

"Fuck me Alpo," I said, looking at the phone. "Fuck me muthafucka." I spread my legs wider when he stood up. "Ohhh shit…" I exploded on my fingers as he put on his boxers.

"Damn I needed that," I said. Alpo turned off the light and I turned off mine. I got under the covers and imagined Alpo and I cuddled up. Before I knew it, I was asleep.

Chapter 13

#CARTEL

I woke up the next morning and finished "The Forty-Eight Laws of Power." Once I was done, I decided to call my father. I hadn't heard from him in a while. I called his cell phone, but he didn't answer. A second later, he returned my call.

"Hello?" I answered.

"What you know good?"

"Calling to check on you. I haven't heard from you in a minute," I said.

"You know I'm maintaining son. How the South been treating you though?"

I hesitated before answering. I didn't like to give my father bad news while he was in prison. He was already in a bad condition physically. I didn't want him to be in a bad condition mentally as well. So, I said, "Everything is love pop. The South couldn't be better." I couldn't tell my father I was in a Gang and deeper in the street than I'd ever been.

"That's great Cartel." He paused, then said, "When I go to the South, the streets pulled me in like quicksand. It was too much going on that I wasn't prepared for. I was just running with the flow. Then I began focusing on myself a little more. Because I was so busy helping others, I didn't realize I was putting myself on pause. Now, I didn't stop helping people. I just started giving more verbal help than financial help. 'Cause sometimes, verbal wisdom can be better than money."

My pops and I talked for almost an hour. For some reason, it felt like he was sending me a message. Everything he spoke about was actually going on in my life. And I hadn't told him my situation. Then I remembered Ms. Anna May telling me to listen to my father and Dough, and how the ancestors would send messages through them.

After talking to my father, I met up with Santana and we picked up Wayne from his house in Darlington, which was only fifteen minutes away. From there we went to De'Asia's bond hearing.

Inside the Courtroom, De'Asia never looked my way. I wanted to tell her that everything would be ok. But she never gave me the chance. De'Asia told the Judge and the family members of the victim that she was sorry, and she wished the victim well. But the family didn't forgive her. They told the Judge that De'Asia was a flight risk as well as a threat to society.

De'Asia tried to defend herself, but the Judge didn't go for it. She denied De'Asia's bond and sent her back to her cell. De'Asia's head dropped for a second, then she lifted it back up. She looked at me for a second, but she didn't smile or nod, she just looked. Something was going on and I needed to find out what it was.

"Santana, hold up," I said. I walked over to one of the Officers who sent De'Asia to the back. "Hey, I'm the defendant's brother. Is it possible I can see her for a second?" I asked.

"Sure. Wait right here." The Officer left the Courtroom and walked through a wooden door. I was finally about to see my woman. I knew she needed to see me, touch me. She also needed to hear me tell her that I was here with her. The Officer returned a minute later, without De'Asia.

"Sir, your sister said she doesn't want to see anyone."

"What?" I asked. Maybe she didn't know it was me, I thought. "Tell her it's Cartel," I said to the Officer.

"She said she doesn't—," I cut the Officer off mid-sentence. "Listen, maybe she thinks I'm her lil' brother. Please just tell her I'm

Cartel. I'm trying to get her a lawyer." The man took a deep breath. "Sir, this is the last time," he said, then he walked back through the wooden door.

My phone was vibrating, but I decided to return all of my calls later. My only concern at the moment was De'Asia. The Officer returned a second time without De'Asia.

"Sir, she said she knows who you are. And she said she doesn't need a lawyer." The Officer's words were like bullets through me. It killed my vibe; it killed my emotions; it killed the next few seconds of my life. I couldn't feel or hear anything for the next thirty seconds. Life didn't seem real. That couldn't be my De'Asia, I thought. I didn't want to accept the fact that she didn't want to see me. But reality would soon sink in.

#SANTANA

On our way out of the Courthouse, I got a call from my cousin.

"Ben, what's good?" I answered. I had called Ben the day before to see

if he could get me a deal on a few kilos.

"I got five blocks cousin. Where you at?" he asked.

"I'm leaving the Courthouse now, but I'll be at Nina's house in

a second."

"That's a go cuz. Let me get everything together and I'll be over

there."

"Ok," I said, then I ended the call. Ben was my mother's

nephew. He was plugged in with some major drug dealers from

Columbia. But he was like the middleman. He would get a few grand

out of the deal, but the people from Columbia really made the profit.

Wayne and I planned on using him until we got plugged in with

something better.

- - -

#DETECTIVE SHAW

Hicks and I were parked in front of a drug dealer's house. His name was Benjamin Parker, but friends and family called him Ben for short. He was well known around the city, so Hicks and I were taking a major risk. We knew once we took his drugs, anything was liable to happen. But I didn't care. I knew we could get multiple kilos from Ben, and if we got enough, we could cool out for a while.

Ben was in the house, while we sat across the street. "Listen. Whenever he comes out, I need you to just hop out and do what you do," I told Hicks. "It's only him, so everything should be easy and smooth. I'll be in the car waiting."

"Alright," Hicks said. Ben lived on the West Side of Florence. The neighborhood wasn't too crowded, but it was empty, so Hicks wouldn't look out of the ordinary. Especially the way he and I were trained to move. We never used a gun or made it look obvious. We would just approach the drug dealer, show our badge and demand the money and product with the promise of not charging them.

We had been sitting out front for nearly an hour when Ben walked out of the house with two duffle bags. He wore a green and white Coogi outfit with black shades, and white and green Jordans. "Catch him before he gets in the car," I ordered Hicks. He opened the car door and rushed across the street. Hicks didn't dress like a detective, so Ben wouldn't be able to tell what was happening.

I watched from the car as Hicks approached Ben. Hicks said something, then showed him his badge. Ben took off his shades and said something, but I couldn't read his lips. Then he gave Hicks the two duffle bags.

#SANTANA

Wayne, Cartel and I waited at Nina's apartment for my cousin Ben

to show up with the bricks. "How much you think the ticket is Money?"

Wayne asked me.

"I don't know, but I know cuz will work with us," I said. I

called his cell phone, but he didn't answer. West Florence wasn't too

far away, so I knew he should've been at Nina's apartment by now. I

waited another ten minutes, then I called his cell phone again. But he

still didn't answer.

"You sure your cousin aint playing no games?" Cartel asked,

growing impatient.

"Nah. Cuz really about business," I said. Seconds later, Ben

pulled up talking on the phone. "That's him right there," I said, seeing

him through the window. He got out of the S.U.V. and walked inside. I

could tell he was mad.

"Diane, he's a tall white guy. Yeah, I know he works there. No,

he couldn't have been on duty. He got black hair." Ben paced the living

room floor as he explained a few more things to a woman named Diane

over the phone. "Send the picture," Ben said. He was still pacing the

floor.

Then a photo came up on his phone. He stopped and looked at it. "No, not him. This guy had a tat on his left hand. A real small tat," Ben explained. Then another photo came through. "Yeah, that's him Diane. Send all the info on that cracker," Ben spat. "Alright." Ben hung up.

"Cuz, you good?" I asked.

"Hell nah. This damn Detective roll on me and took ten damn bricks. I was bringing you five and taking the rest somewhere else," Ben told us.

"A detective?" I asked.

"Yeah. But he promised not to charge me. Basically, he's a crooked-ass cop tryna come up. But he fucked with the wrong muthafucka." Ben looked at his phone. "Randy Hicks, Seven-Twenty-Seven Second Loop Road. Wife is Liz Hicks. They have one child together," Ben read the information from his phone. He knew everything about the Detective. His name, family, age, criminal record and how long he was a Detective. "You gon' help me get these bricks back or not?" Ben asked.

"You already know what's up cuz," I said.

#CARTEL

I sat in the backseat of Ben's S.U.V., gripping my 357. I was
hoping the mission would be a clean getaway. I planned on going inside
the house, getting what belonged to Ben and the Gang, then leaving.
Santana sat beside me with a black 380, while Wayne sat in the
passenger seat.

Ben made a left, turning onto Second Loop Road. The Detective
lived in a nice neighborhood. I took my green bandana from around my
head and used it to cover my face. "He live right here," Ben said as we
drove past a brick house.

"Circle the block," Wayne said. Ben made a right at the corner.
Once we were on the back street, Ben stopped. "We going to park the
whip right here and walk around," he said. "I don't want them to see
my car."

"Alright. Park beside the Benz," Santana said, pointing to a red
Benz. Ben parked and we all got out of the car. Santana covered his
face with his green bandana and Wayne did the same. Ben looked at us
three and decided to cover his face. He reached in the backseat and

grabbed a white shirt. He covered his face so that no one could identify him.

We all crept through a huge yard and jumped the gate. I touched my vial in my pocket and hoped that no one noticed us creeping in the night. We jumped another gate and landed in the Detective's yard. A light was on in the house, so we knew someone was home.

I was following Santana when a small dog began to bark. "Roof! Roof!" I looked at the dog running around the yard. I wanted to snatch its ass up. Instead, I ducked and rushed to the side of the house. The other three hid as well. The dog continued to bark and run wild.

The back door opened, and a little boy walked out with a bag of dog food. "Sit boy, sit," the boy said to the dog. Ben came out of hiding and snatched the white boy up. The boy kicked, trying to fight free, but he wasn't strong enough. Ben covered the boy's mouth with his hand to muffle his voice. Then he ran in the back door, and we all followed and locked the door behind us.

"Tim, give Lady some water, too," the mother said from the bedroom. Wayne nodded at me and tiptoed towards the voice. The inside of the Detective's house was nice. As I was going toward the bedroom, I noticed a photo on the wall. It was of two men. I didn't know one of the men, but I recognized the other man as Kelly's husband. Then I remembered that he was also a Detective.

I continued to the bedroom with the 357 in my hand. The bedroom door was cracked a little. The only light that came from the room was the T.V. Without thinking twice, I entered the room, and flipped the light switch on.

"Ahhh!" The lady yelled, but she stopped when I pointed the gun at her face. "Just chill ma. Everything's good. Get up and come to the living room," I said, lowering the gun.

"Everything's under the bed. Just don't kill us," the lady pleaded as she got out of the bed.

"I'm not going to kill you. Just follow our instructions," I said. She exited the room and I followed with my gun pointed to her back. She walked to the living room and ran to her son who was sitting on the couch.

"Tim, oh my God! Are you ok? Are you ok?" his mother asked, hugging him.

"I'm ok ma," Tim assured his mother.

"Where's your husband?" Ben asked the woman.

"He'll be home soon, but please don't hurt him. Everything is under the bed," she cried.

"Cartel, go…" Wayne stopped himself when he realized he had said my name. I looked at Wayne as if he'd lost is mind. "Damn Money," Wayne said, cussing himself for the mistake. He looked at me, then at the lady and her son, who were still hugging on the couch.

I knew he would have to kill them both. We couldn't trust them to keep my name a secret. I looked at Wayne, and Wayne looked at Santana. I couldn't watch the child die, so I turned around and walked to the bedroom. I fell to me knees to look under the bed when two shots went off. "Pop! Pop!"

I closed my eyes and took a deep breath. I kept them closed for five seconds and then opened them. I searched under the bed and found two blue duffle bags. I unzipped one and looked at the stacks of money. Off to the side, I noticed some pictures. I grabbed the photos and flipped through them.

I recognized Richboy's face. He was holding a gun as he entered a house. There were other pictures, but I didn't know the people. I placed the pictures back inside the bag and zipped it up.

"Money hurry up!" Santana yelled. I took the duffle bags and ran back into the living room. As I entered the room, I tried not to look at the two bodies on the couch.

"You got it?" Ben asked.

"It aint no dope, but there's mad cash," I said.

"Fuck!" Ben spat. "Alright, let's ride yo," he said. I gave Santana one duffle bag and we all went out the same way we came in.

Chapter 14

#DETECTIVE SHAW

Hicks was going through a lot. His wife and son were dead. I knew he needed some time to himself, so I wasn't trying to mix his problems with mine. My only concern was getting these kilos to Rich Squad. I also wanted to know who murdered Hicks' family because whoever murdered them also snatched the photos of Rich Squad running into the weed man's house. But it would be damn near impossible to pinpoint who did it. Hicks and I had so much bad blood on the streets; it could've been anybody.

I called Richboy and he answered. "Talk to me," he said. Richboy knew whenever I called, I had something for him.

"Meet me at Thunderbird in an hour. I got ten turkeys for you," I said. 'Turkey' was a code hustlers used for crack or coke in Florence, and when I said ten, Richboy knew I wasn't talking about ten grams.

"How much a pop?" he asked.

"Five a pop." Five grand each, totaling fifty grand, which left me with twenty-five grand after I split it with my partner.

"Deal." Richboy and I hung up the phone to prepare ourselves for the transaction. Although I didn't have the photos anymore, I couldn't admit that to Rich Squad. That would give them the power, and if anybody had power, it would always be me.

I sat on the edge of my bed while my wife slept. I took the kilos from the original bags, then placed them inside another bag. I was zipping the bag closed when my cell phone went off, waking my wife. She rolled over and wiped her eyes. I answered my phone, "Hello?"

It was Hicks. "You sold the stuff yet?" he asked, in a low tone.

"I'm making the move now. I'll stop by your place when I'm done."

"Ok. 'Cause whoever broke into my house stole all the money I had saved up. I mean, they took every dime," he added.

"Alright, give me a couple of hours brother." I ended the call and placed my cell phone in my pocket. "Baby, I'm scared," my wife said, standing to her feet.

"Scared of what?" I asked.

"You know what happened to Hicks could've happened to us," she said.

"Listen, I don't have time to hear this right now, Kelly. I got mad money to make. Hell, it could've been you, but it wasn't. Be grateful."

"But I'm..." I cut her off.

"Kelly, I don't want to hear that shit! If you're scared, then get the fuck out! All you do is sit up in here and suck up my damn money anyway," I spat. Before she could respond, I grabbed the kilos and stormed past her.

- - -

#RICHBOY

Deebo and I got to Thunderbird at about a quarter to four. I called Shaw and he answered on the third ring. "I'm down the street, pulling up in one minute," he said.

"Ok."

"Just get out and grab the bag out of my backseat. Put the money in its place," he said.

"Say no more."

"Do I have to count money?" he asked.

"Now, why would you have to do that?" I asked.

"I'm just asking." I ended the call. "Bro, when he pull up, take the bag to his backseat and get the turkey," I told Deebo.

"Bet," he said.

Minutes later, Shaw turned in the parking lot and parked beside me. Deebo waited for a second, then did as I told him. Once the transaction was done, I drove out of the parking lot and called Alpo. "Alpo, where you at bro?" I asked.

"Just now getting up," he said.

"Well, the blocks just came in. I'm about to go to Brunson now."

"I'm on my way," he said, then hung up.

I swerved down Highway 52, feeling like the man. Every man in the hood lived to meet a plug. They couldn't wait until the day they had ten kilos of cocaine in the backseat. I stopped at the light and rolled my window down so that the Carolina air could come in. While I was at the light, Santana pulled up beside me in the next lane. He looked over at me, then I smashed the gas and entered North Florence.

#DE'ASIA

I laid in my bunk, staring at the wall. I couldn't believe that the Judge denied my bond. Everything seemed like it was becoming worse by the day. What would my father do? I wondered to myself. How would he handle this situation? Somehow, my father always seemed to have everything under control. He was never down or caught in a maze too long. He always thought his way out.

I was still thinking when Nova jumped down from the top bunk. "Girl, you can't do your time like that. You better read or something to keep your minds off things," she said.

In the County Jail, we didn't have a T.V. or radios to occupy our minds. The only T.V. was outside our cells, but we only went outside our cells for two hours out of the day. One hour in the morning, and one at night. Within those two hours, we had to shower, play games and use the phone. I didn't use the phone, so I showered and played spades with Nova and two other females.

"What books do you have?" I asked Nova.

"I got the entire Cartel series." The name Cartel made my stomach turn. "What else you have?" I asked. I was trying to avoid the Cartel books, but Nova wouldn't let me.

"De' just check it out. If you don't like it, then I'll get you something else." Nova threw the book on my bed. I picked it up and looked at the cover. Then I opened it and began reading. I read the first chapter, then the second and third. Before I knew it, I was deep into the book.

- - -

#ALPO

Once everybody was on Brunson Street, we all split the ten kilos equally. That left everyone with two kilos a piece. Although I had just two kilos, I knew I could whip that into three and a half kilos of crack. I made a mental note to cook the coke later that night. In the meantime, I needed some weed to relax my mind,

"Lil-Baby, you know where some bud at?" I asked.

"Kilo got some good shit," Lil-Baby said. Kilo pulled out an ounce of light green marijuana. It was stuffed in a Ziploc bag. He slid it across the table to me.

"How much you want for this?" I asked, putting it to my nose.

"You good bro," Kilo said. His phone went off then, and he answered it. "Talk to me. Alright, I'm coming now fam." He hung up and looked at Richboy. "Rich, take me to make this play real fast," he said.

"Damn, you need to get your own whip," Richboy joked.

"Don't worry. Ima cop something nice real soon. You better believe that," Kilo said, following my brother out the door. For some reason, I liked Kilo. He had goals and ambition. Deebo was a nice kid, too, but he was more of a follower to me. That wasn't a bad thing if used correctly because everyone needed to be a good follower to be a good leader. I wasn't sure if Richboy was a good leader. He knew how to get a dollar, but he didn't know what to do with the dollar.

"Deebo, you in school?" I asked. I could tell I had caught him off guard with the question.

"Um… well I aint been going to school lately. But yeah, I'm in school," he said.

"Everybody hustles drugs," I started, "because it's easy to do. All you have to do is cop some crack and sell it. But you ever ask yourself why people be hustlin' for twenty and years or more?" I asked.

"Nah," Deebo replied.

"That's because they don't know what to do with the money. They hustle and don't even know what they're hustling for. A real hustler know what he's hustling for, and once he accomplish whatever he's hustling for, then he pass the game onto the next man," I explained.

Deebo nodded his head like he was soaking up the knowledge. "You smarter than I thought," Lil-Baby joked.

"Nigga, I taught you everything you know," I said. I kicked it with the crew for a while, then I left to go chill with Sonya at the hospital.

Chapter 15

#CARTEL

After taking the money from the Detective, we split the seventy-five grand four ways. Santana's cousin, Ben, also told us that he'd supply us with the bricks. He said he did rounds every Friday, so we needed to put our orders in by Thursday morning. The price wasn't as good as Rico's was, but it was good enough to make some money. Money Bag Gang was finally back in operation.

Wayne held a meeting in the Projects and informed the Gang that we had a new plug. While at the meeting, Wayne threw the photos of Rich Squad on the table. Santana and I already knew about the photos, but Trouble, Kapo, Cam, Turk and Juvie didn't know.

"These photos were taken by a Detective," Wayne said. Juvie grabbed them and flipped through them. "As you can see, the Detective had evidence that Rich Squad robbed and murdered Zack and his family," Wayne explained. Juvie passed the photos to Kapo.

"That explains how Vick got in there," Kapo added, looking at the photos.

"Yeah, Vick got killed in the process," Wayne said.

"But the question is why the Detective didn't arrest them?" Juvie asked.

"Bingo!" Wayne said, looking at Juvie. "Now let me remind y'all. This is the same Detective that took Ben's dope and didn't arrest him," Wayne said.

"So, what's he doing with the dope?" Trouble asked.

"My theory is he sells the dope he gets from drug raids. That would explain how a Detective had seventy-five grand in cash just laying around," Wayne said.

"And that's where Rich Squad would get their dope from," Juvie connected the dots.

"Exactly," Wayne said. Everything added up. It didn't take rocket science to figure it out.

"But that's none of our business," Kapo said.

"Nah, but we can keep these pictures. They may come in handy someday," Wayne said.

After the meeting, Juvie and I stepped outside. "How the fam doing?" I asked Juvie.

"They're good. Stuff just been a lil' slow without a plug. My ol' lady was really taking care of a nigga," Juvie admitted.

"Well, we have a plug now."

"True. But how De'Asia?" Juvie asked.

"Money, I don't even know. Shorty won't even talk to a nigga."

"She probably going through a lot. Her pops died, and now she locked up," Juvie paused, then he continued, "she probably just needs some time."

"You're right, Money." Juvie and I were still talking when Kelly drove into the Projects. "That's your people right there?" Juvie asked, knowing Kelly loved to get dope from me.

"Yeah, hold up," I said. Kelly parked beside Santana's truck. I walked over and got into the passenger seat. "Kelly, how you been?" I asked. I could tell she had been crying. Her eyes were red and puffy, and she looked like she hadn't slept in days.

"A lot been going on, Cartel," she mumbled. "I just can't do it no more," she added. She held back her tears and bit her bottom lip. "I packed my stuff, and now I'm going to get my shit together," she spat, nodding to the backseat. I looked back at her packed luggage.

"How you goin' to survive with no money?" I asked, knowing she didn't have a job.

"You need to ask my husband that?" She cracked a smile.

"No, you didn't," I said, laughing.

"Hell yeah I did. He done robbed drug dealers for years. He got plenty money. I was his wife long enough to get something off the top," she said.

"Well, what you going to do?" I asked.

"I'm going to New York to get myself together and maybe start a business or something." I couldn't believe Kelly was doing it, but I was proud of her.

"So, you aint come to get no turkey?" I asked.

"Nope. I got a dime left, and I'm trying to make it my last." I smiled and gave her a hug. Kelly was a good woman, and she deserved a whole lot more. "Thank you for everything, Cartel," she said. I didn't do much for Kelly, but sometimes just listening and understanding someone means a lot to them.

"You're welcome. Call me when you get yourself together," I said.

"I will."

- - -

#DE'ASIA

The book Nova let me read had my mind on some mafia-type shit. It gave me visions. Maybe I could be the first Queen Pen in South Carolina. I could run my own operation exactly how my father ran his gang. But I wanted to be bigger than a gang. I wanted to be in charge of my own empire. I smiled to myself as I pictured myself in a candy apple red Mazerati, with black leather seats.

I was still daydreaming when the Correctional Officer opened up our cell doors. I put on my slippers and rushed out to the phones. I needed to get in contact with Parish. I dialed her number, but she declined my call. I called back two more times, but she still didn't answer.

"What the fuck!" I slammed the phone on the hook. Everybody around looked at me like I was insane. I left the phone and joined Nova and her homegirl, Trina, at the card table.

"De', you alright?" Nova asked.

"Yeah, I'm good," I said.

"Nova, your lawyer here," the Correctional Officer said.

"This nigga better have some good news," Nova said, standing to her feet. "Trina, watch my homie and make sure she don't kill herself," Nova joked as she walked off.

"Nova a trip," Trina giggled. Trina was a cool girl from Darlington, South Carolina. She was arrested a few weeks ago for prostitution and she couldn't post bail.

"Yeah, she is a trip," I agreed.

"I hope they go ahead and let her go. This jail shit is for the birds," Trina said, shuffling a deck of playing cards.

"How much your bond is?" I asked.

"All I need is a grand."

"A grand?"

"Yup." I couldn't believe Trina couldn't afford to bail out. I looked around the pod and wondered how many other females were in jail and couldn't pay their bond. Ten minutes later, Nova returned smiling.

"What he say?" I asked.

"He said he going to talk to the solicitor today. And he said it's looking real good." Nova sat down and her smile faded. "I don't even know what Ima do when I get out there De'." Nova dropped her head. "I got to start all the way over."

Trina put her hand on Nova's knee. "You can do it, Nova," Trina said, trying to lift Nova's spirit. Struggling was normal to them, but all I knew was money. I didn't know anything about hard times and prostitution. All Nova and Trina had to do was go get the money. At that moment, a plan came to my mind. I knew who had the money, and I knew the perfect way to get it.

"I got a plan, Nova," I said, smiling from ear to ear. Nova looked up with hope in her eyes. "But if y'all going to be with me, then we got to have loyalty. Without that, we aint got nothing," I said.

"De'Asia, if this shit is about getting paid, then count me in," Trina said.

"Me too, De'," Nova said.

I looked at Nova and Trina seriously. "Alright look. I know the ins and outs to that Money Bag Gang shit," I whispered. "All we gotta do is…"

Chapter 16

#RICHBOY

After selling crack all day and night, I snuck to the motel with Jemilla. Jemilla was a female a muthafucka would clown you about. She was the Northside whore, but God knows she had the best pussy in all of Florence. I stroked deep and long. "Damn, this pussy good," I said, gripping the sheets. I could feel her pussy juice sliding down my inner thigh. She spread her legs wider, then she palmed my butt cheeks, guiding me deeper.

"Yes… yes," she moaned. She closed her eyes, enjoying the pleasure. When she opened her eyes, I exploded inside her wetness. My body went limp, and I rolled over on my back. "Damn," I said, trying to catch my breath.

But Jemilla wasn't done. She ducked under the cover and swallowed my dick. "Fuck," I grunted. Her head was going up and down like a bobble head. "Uumm," she moaned like she was eating ice cream. It wasn't long before I was back in her pussy, going for round two.

Jemilla and I had sex for two hours. Once we were done, I laid on my back with her head on my chest. I ran my fingers through her hair, while she played with my balls. "Rich, have you ever thought about moving away?" she asked out of nowhere.

"Nah, not really. Why you ask?"

"I don't want to be on Brunson Street forever," she paused like she was thinking of the perfect place to be. Then she said, "I always wanted to move somewhere like Georgia or Florida. You know what I mean?"

"Yeah," I agreed. Except I couldn't imagine moving away from all of my family and friends. Florence was all I ever knew. But I guess moving out of the hood was what it was all about. "Maybe one day I'll pack up and leave," I said.

"You got mad potential, Richboy. I can tell you have a good heart deep inside, but the streets force you to hide that part."

"What are you talking about?" I smiled. She looked into my eyes but didn't smile back at me. She kissed my lip. I sucked on her bottom lip and stuck my tongue in her mouth. My dick stood back at attention. It was throbbing to feel Jemilla's insides. She climbed back on top of me, and we went for round three.

#ALPO

Lil-Baby and Richboy were gone, so Deebo, Kilo and I held down the trap. We ran up and down Brunson Street all night. We all stayed up until the following morning. The money had us up like we were on a gallon of black coffee. I sat on the porch counting money while Deebo and Kilo passed a blunt back and forth.

"Richboy up mad early," Deebo said, as he watched Richboy turn into the yard.

He stepped out of the Range Rover and slammed the door back. "Damn, y'all pulled an all-nighter?" Richboy asked, dapping us up.

"Yeah, the dope aint gonna sell itself," I said. Seconds later, Jemilla turned into her yard, which was across the street from the Peter Rabbit store. All eyes were on her booty as she got out of her Honda. "Girl know she thick," Deebo said.

"Yeah, but I know that pussy ran through. Some niggas from the Projects ran a train on her. Them muthafuckas were taking turns on her," Kilo said, watching her booty clap. Richboy turned his attention to Kilo. "How you know that?" he asked.

"Well, that's what the word is," Kilo said.

"That's what's wrong with y'all young bucks. Spreading rumors y'all don't even know."

"Yeah, 'cause muthafuckas be lying on they dick," Deebo agreed, passing his brother the blunt.

"I feel ya," Kilo said.

I stuffed my money in my pocket and stood to my feet. "I'll be back later. I got to catch some z's. Then Ima stop by the hospital to chill with Sonya," I said.

"How sis doin'?" Richboy asked.

"She up and talking. They releasing her in a few more days."

"That's good," Richboy said. I pound them up and went to my apartment to get some sleep.

#RICHBOY

I tried my best to get Jemilla off my mind, but I couldn't. I texted her and asked if I could see her that night. A minute passed, and then she said it was cool. I smiled to myself and placed my phone in my pocket.

"Yo, Rich. You tryna sell a whole block?" Kilo asked.

"You out of turkey?" I asked.

"No, I just want to break all my shit down."

"Oh, yeah. I got a block. But I need twenty-five though." Kilo said something to whoever was on the other end of the phone, then he ended the call. "Come on. The sale is in West Florence," Kilo said, standing to his feet.

"Deebo, hold the trap down until we come back," I said. I rushed inside the house and grabbed a kilo and placed it inside a grocery bag.

Kilo and I got into my Range Rover. I threw the kilo in the backseat and backed out of the yard. "You know the person we serving?" I asked as we passed Jemilla's house.

"Yeah, he used to play ball with me at Wilson," Kilo said. Wilson was a high school located in West Florence.

"That's what's up," I said, making a right onto Darlington Street. West Florence was known for selling crack. Real hustlers and money makers ran through the two hoods on the Westside. They were known as 'the Bottom' and 'Gladstone'.

"Make this right," Kilo said. I slowed down and turned right on Coit Street. "It's the fourth house on the right." I parked in front of the house. Kilo made a call and told the person on the other end to come outside. A short man walked outside, dressed in a blue and green Coogi outfit. He made his way across the lawn and got into the backseat.

"What's good family?" the man asked. Kilo dapped him up and nodded to the grocery bag.

"Everything's good big bro. The cash straight?" Kilo asked. The man looked inside the bag and then handed over the cash.

"It's all there family." The man closed the grocery bag tight.

"Thanks for the business," Kilo said. I took the cash from Kilo and thumbed through it.

"You already know what's up," the man said as he got out of the car.

"Put this in the glove box," I said to Kilo as I passed him the cash. He took it and stuffed it into the glove box. There was nothing like selling drugs. All a person had to do was get the product and sell it. With the right mindset, he or she could be a million dollars strong.

- - -

#DETECTIVE SHAW

I paced my living room floor and dialed Kelly's number. She kept sending me to voicemail. "Fuck!" I threw my cell phone against the wall. I needed a bust bad. Kelly took my money and skipped town on me. I pulled out a cigarette and lit it. I needed to calm my nerves before I left the house.

After smoking the cigarette, I picked my phone back up off the floor and called Hicks. "Hello?" he answered.

"Yo, where are you?" I asked.

"Shaw, I'm busy right now."

"Man, it's an emergency," I spat.

"Um… umm… I'll call you back in a second Shaw." I hung up the phone even angrier than before. I needed Hicks for the bust. I couldn't pull it off by myself. I was still pacing the floor when he called back. "Yeah," I answered.

"I'm at the house."

"Alright, I'm on my way." I hung up and rushed over to Hicks' house. He got in the car looking like he lost fifty pounds. "Man, my wife wiped me out," I said.

"What?" Hicks asked, confused.

"Kelly took my money and skipped town on me," I said, making myself clear.

"Damn Shaw. I'm sorry to hear that." I backed out of his driveway. "Shaw?" Hicks mumbled.

"Yeah?"

"I... I think Ima make this my last bust," he said. I looked at Hicks like he was retarded. He knew I couldn't let him leave. There was no way he could leave me at a time like this.

"Hicks, you're just down right now and talking suicide. You'll be better tomorrow," I said, hoping he caught the hint in the word 'suicide'.

Chapter 17

#CARTEL

Although Ben kept his word and delivered the kilos like he said he would, something didn't feel right when I woke up. For the first time in a while, I called my mother.

"Hello," she answered. Her voice still sounded sweet as candy.

"How ya been ma?" I asked.

There was a long silence, then she said, "Cartel?"

"Yes, ma, it's me." I knew she couldn't believe it was me calling.

"I'm good, son. How about yourself?"

"I great. Carolina's taking care of me," I said.

"Are you staying out of trouble?" she asked.

"Yeah." It felt good hearing my mother's voice. We talked for a little while longer, then we ended the conversation. I got myself together and got dressed. I grabbed my 357 and my vial, then left the house. As I was on my way to the county jail, Santana called.

"Yo," I answered.

"Money where you at?" he asked.

"On my way to the jail house. Ima put a few dollars on De'Asia's book."

"Oh, well the Gang at the spot. Everything's back popping," Santana said.

"Alright. Give me about an hour." I ended the call and turned into the jail parking lot. I left the car running while I put a grand on De'Asia's book. I promised myself I would do the same thing the following week.

- - -

#DE'ASIA

As bad as I didn't want Nova to leave, I knew she had to. She threw a few items in a bag and then she threw the bag over her shoulder. Trina stood there with tears in her eyes.

"Girl, wipe yo eyes. I'm coming back to bail you out. Just give me a week," Nova said.

"Ima miss you though," Trina cried.

"Stop all that soft shit," I said. Trina rolled her eyes at me, then we had a big group hug.

"You two hold that shit down," Nova whispered.

"Don't worry about us. You just make sure you stick to the plan," I said.

Nova stepped back. "I got that covered," Nova said.

"Say no more. I'm goin' to call the number you gave me around this time tomorrow," I said.

"Bet." Nova hugged us one last time, then she followed the Correctional Officer out of the pod door.

"I'm glad them crackers dropped her murder charge," Trina said.

"Me too."

The second Nova was released, I got a new cellmate. I had to admit, she was pretty. She was brown skin, with a nice shape and stood about five foot seven. She wore her hair straight down her back. "What's your name?" I asked her.

"Rya. And yours?" she asked.

"I'm De'Asia."

- - -

#SANTANA

Being the captain of Money Bag Gang didn't make me feel any different. The Gang respected me with or without the rank. I sat in the spot and observed how the Gang conducted business. After a while, I realized that Rico had trained them well. Money was moving in nonstop. A little past noon, Cartel stepped into the apartment.

"Money, how you?" I asked.

"I'm lovely," he replied, dapping the Gang up. He sat down on the couch beside Trouble. I pulled a Dutch from my pocket and bust it down the middle. Then I filled the inside with kush. I was about to spark the blunt when I realized it was Nina's birthday.

"Damn, Cartel, roll with me fast," I said, rushing out the door. Cartel rushed out behind me.

"What's up bro?" he asked, catching up with me.

"It's Nina's birthday. I almost forgot." We walked over to Nina's apartment and stepped inside.

"Where the birthday girl at?" I yelled. Cartel closed the door.

"Nigga, you forgot," Nina said, walking from the kitchen in a bathrobe.

"No, I didn't." I pulled out a wad of cash and gave it to her.

"Thanks, but you still forgot," Nina said, rolling her eyes.

"How can I forget?" I asked with a smirk.

"He did forget," Cartel laughed, handing Nina a bundle of hundreds. I looked at Cartel, then at Nina. "Ok, fine. But I did remember, though. You didn't have to remind me," I said, trying to defend myself.

We all burst out laughing. "Just be ready for tonight. Everybody going out," I said.

- - -

#PARISH

I hadn't left my aunt's house in a few days. The world didn't have anything to offer me but drama. Every day I smoked my life away. I drowned my mind with marijuana to escape reality. De'Asia called me every day, but I always declined her call. I figured she was the reason I was in the situation I was in. if she would have never drove the car into Sonya, then Alpo would have been back by my side. He always came back.

I was smoking on my third blunt of the day when I decided to check to see if Alpo made it home. I turned on my phone and looked at the camera. I couldn't believe my eyes. Sonya was out of the hospital, and she was in my man's bed.

- - -

#CARTEL

The entire Gang was in the club celebrating Nina's birthday, except Kapo and Cam. They decided to stay back and collect the late-night money. That's something I would've done if it wasn't Nina's money. We all sat in V.I.P. popping bottles.

"Baby girl, you know I don't drink," Juvie said. "But you can have a drink for me," he added. Nina took the bottle and turned it up. Rich Homie Quan's voice blasted through the speakers. Santana took the liquor bottle from Nina.

"You better slow down," he said. Nina pouted like a baby, but Santana stood his ground.

"I know y'all say y'all like Auntie and Nephew," I said, smiling, "but y'all will make a perfect couple."

"Cartel, don't start," Santana said.

"Santana wouldn't know what to do with me," Nina said, looking at Santana. Everybody stopped what they were doing and looked at Santana, who was shocked by Nina's reply. But that didn't stop him from tonguing her down. They kissed like they were in love.

"Yeah!" Wayne cheered. The whole V.I.P. section started clapping. That was a moment I would never forget. That's when I realized that we were really family. We all partied until the club lights came on.

"Y'all don't have to go home, but y'all got to get the hell out of here!" the DJ yelled over the loudspeaker. I looked around for Juvie because I knew that he and I were the only two sober ones. I found him talking to his baby mother against the wall. "Yo Juvie!" I yelled.

He looked at me and walked over. "What's good Money?"

"I'm out. Where's Wayne? I know he probably can't drive home," I said.

"Wayne with me and Trouble. I'll drop 'em off."

"Say no more," I said. Santana stumbled over.

"You make sure you get him home," Juvie laughed.

"Where's Nina?" Santana slurred.

"Nina left about twenty minutes ago," Juvie said.

"She was drunk?" I asked.

"Of course she was drunk. But not to the point where she couldn't drive," Juvie said.

"Alright. Let us get out of here. I'll catch you tomorrow, Money," I said. I dapped Juvie up, then I led Santana out the club. I helped him into the passenger seat of his F-150. I took the keys from his pocket and got into the driver's seat. "I aint never drove this big boy," I said, driving slowly out of the parking lot.

"Don't crash my shit," Santana said, laying back in the seat. Santana's phone was going off, but he didn't answer. Whoever was calling was doing it back-to-back. "You aint going to answer the line?" I asked, making a right turn.

"It aint nobody but a fiend," he said with his eyes closed. I made another turn and stopped at a red light. Santana's phone stopped ringing, but then my phone went off. I pulled it out and answered it.

"Hello?"

It was crackhead Mike. "Cartel, somebody killed Kapo and Cam. The Police everywhere." Crackhead Mike was talking a mile a minute. Then someone else called my phone. I didn't recognize the number. "Hold up Mike," I said. Then I clicked over and listened.

"Cartel." It was a female voice.

"Who this?" I asked.

"Call me whatever you want to call me. But just know you and your partner better come up with half a million or Nina's dead."

"What?" I asked. I put the phone on speaker so Santana could hear.

"Hold up," the lady said. A second later, Nina's voice cracked through the phone. "Cartel, please… please get the… the money."

"Nina!" Santana yelled, but it was too late. The kidnapper was back on the phone. "Like I said, five hundred grand," she said.

"We need time to get that kind of bread," I said. It took everything in my power for me to stay calm.

"I thought y'all were Money Bag?" she laughed. Then said, "Seven hundred and fifty grand. You got three months." Then she hung up.

- - -

#DE'ASIA

The next day, I called Nova and she told me the job was done.

"That's what I'm talking about," I said, smiling from ear to ear.

"And tell Trina to pack up. I'm coming to get her in a minute," Nova said.

"I got you." I wanted to get all the details, but I knew that was impossible on the jail phone.

"Stay strong back there De'. You'll be home soon," Nova said.

"After all I been through, I think I'm qualified as a strong woman!" I said.

"You are," Nova agreed. I ended the call feeling better than ever. I was finally putting my plan in motion. "I love you dad," I said to myself. I knew he was looking down on me and smiling…

THE END

Crossed Out is an exciting and action-packed novel that follows Cartel and De'Asia thrilling journey. The first Part will take you on an emotional journey with Cartel and De'Asia. As the story progresses, you will be rooting for them through each challenge. The ending of the first part will leave you eagerly awaiting the next installment - so make sure to stay tuned for Part 2!

Submit your opinion on how the story should end in the Amazon review section. Find out if Cartel and De'Asia will succeed in their mission by reading Crossed Out Part 1!

JONES Family TREE

The Jones family is a black family that has been around for generations, and they have a secret that could shatter their world. Vedo is one of the family members, and he has a secret that he's been hiding from them. Unfortunately, his secret ends up causing tragedy in the family, resulting in his brother's death and him being exiled and on the brink of death. Will Vedo survive?

The Jones family's only hope lies in the Clark family, a white family whose forefathers have bonded with the Jones family long ago. Their support saves Vedo from prison, and the killer is eventually found. But it turns out that the killer is none other than the son of the Clark family. Now they must decide if they will prioritize the bond between their families or stand by their son. What will the Clarks choose, the family bond or their own son? Find out in this captivating tale of courage and determination.

The Jones Family Tree offers readers a thrilling adventure and insight into the struggle between black and white families during America's history. It delves into the secrets between the two families and how those secrets can cause devastating consequences. It also looks at the power of family bonds and how even in the face of adversity, a family can come together and support each other. Through Vedo's journey, readers will learn about resilience, loyalty, and courage, as well as gain a better understanding of the issues faced by African Americans during this time.

2022 © Ling Publishing LLC
PO box 210596 Columbia, SC 29210
www.Lingpublishing.com

LingBooks

JONES Family TREE

JABRIEL CRAWFORD & KEITH WEEKS

Made in the USA
Middletown, DE
30 September 2023

39509968R00126